One

Tim Branch was a wealthy man. He was rich in both cash and non-cash assets. Being a man who ran a multi-million-dollar company, he was always busy. He was in his mid-forties and unmarried, without children. Tim loved children and the idea of a happy life. He found delight in the prospect of a life with a family. He wished to get married and someday have a family of his own, something he had always cherished.

Tim usually began his day by taking a good morning bath in his beautifully decorated jacuzzi. He usually slept on a king-sized bed alone. He made himself an early breakfast before putting on his clothes and getting ready for work. He wished to have a woman who would prepare his breakfast and meals in the normal traditional family setting someday, such as those generally seen in the culture of the mormons and the native Americans. An ordinary American woman would not be the ideal wife for him.

But this morning was not usual. Being in his mid-forties, he supposed that it was gradually becoming late for him to have and raise children. Tim had decided that this was the right time to get married. A typical American woman was not in his mind. He thought they were full of it. They want their husband to cook for them and demand equal rights with men. They could easily divorce their husbands and rip them apart.

1

Tim's business demanded that he traveled back and forth to the United States. He was a frequent flier and had earned the frequent flyer discount from some airlines. He traveled to the Philippines on regular business trips, and there he had met a beautiful young Philippine woman who worked as a housekeeper in the hotel he stayed at. She was in her mid-twenties, about five feet three inches tall; she had slender, long, blond hair and dark eyes. Her perfect-sized breasts were still firm, her thighs were curved and her buttocks stuck out gracefully. She worked humbly, cleaning the guest rooms. She was fluent in English as well.

At around 2pm, he heard a knock on his door. He got up from his bed and sat upright.

"Housekeeping" the knocker said.

"Yes, come in" Tim replied

She opened the door all the way and put a stopper against the door.

When she walked inside his room, Tim gazed at her lustfully and said, "Hello girl, how are you?"

"I'm fine," she said.

"You are so beautiful," Tim replied.

She laughed happily, starring at the ceiling top. She seemed to feel so good about the compliment.

"Thank you."

"What's your name?"

"Angelina... but my friends call me Angie."

"Can I call you Angie then?"

"Yes, I like that."

Tim smiled. "Alright Angie, from now on, I'll call you Angie."

Angelina noticed Tim's foreign accent and figured out that he was not from the Philippines.

"I hope you don't mind me asking... where are you from?"

"I'm from the United States."

"What part?"

"The eastern part of New York. I'm here on a short business trip and hope to return soon."

Angelina thought about America for a moment. She had a family member who lived there and had told her much about the beauties of Manhattan. She always dreamed about coming to the United States. Tim, on the other hand, was much interested in something else.

"Are you married?" Tim asked.

"No, I'm not. In the Philippines, you have more women than men. I'll just wait until I find the perfect man."

Tim stood up and went closer to her. "I am single myself and would love to get married someday."

"Oh great! That's a good idea."

"Perhaps you have found the perfect man. Will you consider marrying me?"

"Ha ha!" she laughed. "You sound and look like a good man. I'd love to. We can go to America and live happily ever after".

"I only have a few days to spend here in the Philippines before I go back to the United States. Why don't you come with me and we can spend the night together and get to know each other more intimately?"

"That sounds good to me. I'll see you by 6.20 p.m. after work. I'll have to go home first so that my father will know that I'm back from work; then, I'll tell him I'm going to spend the night at my friend's house today; then I'll come visit you."

Angelina did just as she said. She went home and came back to Tim's hotel room. They spent the night together. Tim hadn't had sex in a long time now. He enjoyed every minute he spent with Angelina. The next morning, Tim immediately contacted the American consulate in Manila, the capital of Philippines, and extended his stay there for six months. They dated all through the time he was there, and they got to know and trust each other very well. They finally got married, but Angelina would not immediately follow Tim back to the United States. Tim had to return first and then file an application to bring Angelina to the United States as his spouse. This process takes quite some time to process, but can be expedited for a good reason.

Mr. Branch was so excited about his trip this time. He felt his dreams were finally coming true. Tim called his mother Victoria to tell her about his marriage to Angelina. She was very happy to hear that Tim was finally married, although she was absent. When she heard that his wife was of a foreign descent, she was not so excited about it. Tim never told her that he was getting married. Victoria had a disappointing experience with her foreign fiancée from Sweden; as a result, she had become doubtful, suspicious and prejudiced about foreigners who wanted to marry American citizens. She felt Angelina married Tim not out of love, but for her quest to come to America. Nevertheless, she could not persuade Tim to change his mind at that time, for Tim had already fallen in love with Angelina.

After a few months of application, with all the supporting documents of proof of good faith marriage,

Angelina Branch finally obtained a visa to come to the United States of America as the spouse of a U.S. citizen.

It was a busy day at the JFK International Airport for Mr. Branch when Angelina arrived. Tim received her with joy, love and happiness. He was happy that his dream wife was finally here to stay. He breathed a sigh of relief. He felt love was finally here to stay.

"Hello honey! Welcome," Tim said. "I'm happy to be here together with you today."

Tim kissed her gently on the cheek and handed her a long leather winter jacket.

"Here is this leather jacket. I bought it in anticipation that it'll be cold."

"Thanks honey," Angelina said, walking hand-in-hand with Tim toward the taxi line.

"How was your flight?"

"It was quite good, and I enjoyed it. I received good treatment from the attendants. The food was awesome."

She came on first-class ticket paid by Mr. Branch, and so received first class service. Tim and Angelina finally arrived home in East New York and they began living together as husband and wife.

They got into the house and Mr. Branch turned on the television set as Mrs. Branch began to unpack. She sat on the living room and started watching television while Tim arranged her room. He designated a room for her and took her on a little tour around the house, showing the living room, bedrooms, basements and especially the kitchen.

"Is this your cooking stove?" she asked, while staring around the kitchen.

"Yes, sweetheart. This is the stove I used to cook with," Angelina looked at Tim, stunned.

"Do you cook? You are a man, you shouldn't. Never mind, I'm here now. I love to cook".

Tim smiled in appreciation of her proclaimed kitchen talents.

"I'm sure you do. This is quite common with women from a foreign background. That's why I love their style. They cook well for their husbands and children, do their laundry and all house-related works."

Angelina smiled sweetly and said, "Yes, we do. I learned how to cook when I was twelve years old, from my mother. I used to watch her cock tirelessly for my father and hoped to do so for my husband one day".

Tim was glad to hear this. In his heart, he felt his dream had come true.

"My aunt Lisa lives in New York. She came to the United States at the age of sixteen."

"Really?" Tim asked.

"Yes, my mother gave me her number to call her and let her know of my arrival to New York. She will be happy to know that I'm finally here."

"It's a great thing to have a close relative around," Tim replied, handing her the phone. "Give her a call and let me know if she'd need directions to the house".

Angelina took the phone from Tim. It was late in the evening and they had decided it was time to call it a night, so they went to bed.

They woke up together this morning. Tim went to the bathroom for a quick shower, getting ready for work.

Angelina walked toward the bathroom to Tim and said, "What will you like for breakfast?"

Tim pulled over the curtain shower very slightly and said, looking toward Angelina with a smile, "Bacon, egg, cheese, and a cup of coffee will be just fine for me".

Angelina, the good wife, walked toward the kitchen, dressed in her lingerie, and prepared bacon, egg and cheese with a cup of mild, hot coffee, just as Tim wanted it, and brought everything up to the dining table. By the time Tim had finished getting ready for work, his breakfast was ready and waiting. What a difference a wife makes! Usually, Tim would go through the McDonald's drive-through to get his breakfast. He did this regularly in order to get to work on time, as his job demands. His clients are always early, and important business decisions cannot be made in his absence. Things were a little better and faster as he could eat before leaving the house. He was beginning to see some good changes in his life. He was beginning to feel like a man for a change, as a result of his marriage to Angelina.

Tim finished eating, kissed his wife and began walking down the stairway. He felt good and was beginning to fall in love with Angelina.

"I'll let my mom and friends know that you have arrived. Very soon, we'll arrange a welcome party. How's that?"

"That's great, honey. I'm looking forward to that".

They kissed each other. Angelina went back into the house, while Tim walked down toward the garage and drove off to work on his BMW.

Two.

While Tim went to work, Angelina went back to their bedroom. She removed the bed sheets, blankets and pillow cases and went down to the basement section of the house. The washing machine and the dryer were installed in the basement. She laundered and dried the bedspreads, blankets, pillow cases and her husband's underwear and socks. She folded them and took them back upstairs to the room, dressed the bed neatly, then put the socks and the underwear in the appropriate basket located by the dresser as if she were still working in the hotel where Tim had first met her. She took the vacuum cleaner and vacuumed the rooms thoroughly and placed every scattered item in the house in the proper place. Most of the household items were scattered all over the place before she began living with Mr. Branch. Before getting married, Mr. Branch usually left his bed unkempt for days, until he was able to dress them. His dirty clothes were all over the house and kept them all in a small basket until he was ready to launder them. Angelina was ready to make right all the unusual things Tim did when he was single.

She left the bedroom and went over to the living room and thoroughly vacuumed it; then, she wiped clean the television set. They were a little dirty but not so dirty that it would be considered out of the ordinary. Keeping the house clean was important to Mr. Branch, but due to his busy work schedule, he was unable to keep them constantly clean. But this time, he was married to a virtuous woman.

Angelina finished her normal daily housework and sat down on the comfortable recliner chair in the living room and turned on the television set. She scrambled through the channels until she found her favorite show. Angelina loves game shows. She sat watching the television game show called the 'Price is Right'. She loves winning prices and all the excitement that comes with it.

As she sat comfortably watching the shows, she thought it right to call her parents in the Philippines to inform them of her safe arrival to the United States. This was a very good thing to do because her parents were eagerly waiting to hear from her. She picked up the telephone set and dialed her parents' number. Her mother was cooking at that time; so, when her phone rang, she dropped the frying spoon she had in her hand and ran to the phone from the kitchen and answered.

"Hello!" she said, breathing heartily.

Angelina stood up with the cordless phone set in her hand; she walked back and forth inside the living room as she spoke to her mother.

"Hello mom, it's Angelina."

Her mother, out of joy and excitement, said, "Angelina! Angie, Angelina... hello Angelina."

Angelina smiled and subtly said, "Hi mom! How are you and daddy doing? "

"We are all here. Your dad went to work, as usual"

"I'm sure he did. That's fine. When he returns, just let him know that I had called."

"I sure will. That's the first thing I'll tell him when he comes back. He'd be very happy to hear that".

Although her father is poor because of the poor economic condition in the Philippine, he's hardworking and dedicated. An able-bodied man, muscular and strongly built, he has managed to provide for the day-to-day living cost of his family. Taking into consideration the poor economic situation in the Philippines, he is considered a success.

"How about my sister Lucy?"

"Lucy is fine. She just went out with her friend. I believe they went to a neighbor's wedding event".

"How is it over there in America?", her mother continued.

"Mom, America is beautiful. My husband Tim is a good man, a business executive. He's gone to work now. He loves me very much. I intend to call aunt Lisa today or perhaps tomorrow when time permits. But I will call you later on, and I promise to keep in constant touch with all of you and continue to update you with my day-to-day progress".

"Okay, Angelina. Just don't forget us. You know how difficult life is down here."

"No problem, mom," Angelina hung up. She sat down on her recliner chair, smiling, and continued watching her game show. It is apparent that Angelina loves high life.

About fifteen minutes later, the game show ended and Angelina decided to call her aunt. She picked up the phone and dialed Lisa's number. Lisa's phone rang but it went straight to the voice mail. Angelina called right back this time and Lisa answered.

"Hello!"

"Hello? Aunt Lisa? This is Angelina."

"Hi Angelina, where are you calling from?"

Lisa did not identify Angelina's number immediately for she was on another line.

"Hold on just for a moment".

She went back on the other line and told the other caller, "Honey, I'll call you back in a while, I have an important call to take". She hung up.

Lisa reconnected with Angelina and the conversation began.

"Angie, where are you?"

"I'm in New York," she replied.

"In New York? Where?

"I just got here a few days ago, but I am not sure of the address yet. My husband is at work now. I can get it when he returns."

Lisa was astonished when Angelina said "my husband". She paused for a while and said, "Did you say my husband?"

Angelina laughed and said "Yes my husband. We got married in Philippines and my husband filed the necessary documents to bring me here to the United States. He is a business man and is at work as we speak. I am here alone right now. I have just finished cooking and cleaning, so I decided to let you know that I am here."

"Cooking and cleaning. Uh, that's good to hear. Well, I'm at work right now myself and can't talk much longer. But I'm very excited to hear from you".

"Likewise."

"I'll be calling you later and we can arrange to meet at a convenient time".

"I'm looking forward to that". They hung up.

Thirty minutes later, her phone rang and Angelina picked up the phone and answered. That was her husband, Mr. Branch calling. He called to check on her, to make sure she was alright and doing well.

Angelina answered, "Hello? Honey?

"Hello. I just called to check on you. How are you doing?"

"I'm perfectly fine. I had called my mom and aunt."

"Oh great! How are they doing?"

"They are doing just fine. My dad was not at home when I called, neither was my sister. I only spoke to my mom and she was very happy to hear from me. Dad was at work, while my sister had gone to a neighbor's wedding. I also spoke to my aunt and she is very happy to know that I am here. She is equally happy to hear from me".

"This is great news. I am happy to know that they've heard from you. I'll be home pretty soon. I have completed just about all the work I needed to do for the day, and hope to see you soon. I miss you."

"Miss you too. See you shortly." They hung up. Angelina sat back on her chair and continued watching television.

Two hours later, Mr. Branch came back from work. He pulled up to the driveway on his black BMW. Angelina had swept the driveway earlier, and it looked very clean. Mr. Branch was astonished at how neat the driveway was. It was quite a surprise to him, for in the past, he had paid professional lawn movers to clean out the driveway of leaves that constantly fell off the trees. As he pulled up closer, the garage door automatically opened. He drove in and parked his vehicle. He pressed the remote-controlled door locks and his vehicle automatically locked as he began walking upstairs into his house.

Angelina heard the footsteps of someone walking toward the door. She knew that it was Tim and she ran joyfully toward the door to receive him. She opened the door and said, "Hello honey, welcome".

They hugged and kissed each other. They held hands and walked into the house together.

"Wow!" Tim screamed as he saw the big difference a day makes. His bedspreads, pillow cases, underwear all were laundered and kept in order. The front yard was all cleaned. Tim was very appreciative of the work done by his wife. He handed her a rose he had purchased for her. After resting a little while, sitting on his bed, he went straight to the shower to take a bath and they went to bed for the evening.

Three

Mr. Branch woke up late the next morning. He had a good night's sleep with Angelina. As usual, Angelina woke up earlier than Mr. Branch and finished refreshing herself. She cleaned up and prepared the morning breakfast for Mr. Branch. By the time Mr. Branch had woken up, breakfast was already ready. His shoes were perfectly polished and shone. Mrs. Branch had polished them. She wanted Tim to wear a different outfit, not the one he wore yesterday. Tim was in agreement with that. He was very impressed with the treatment he got from his wife and decided he would do something for her.

"Angie..."

"Yes honey?"

"I have a suggestion".

"Tell me".

"Would you like to further your education by attending college?"

"I've always thought about that. My dream has always been to graduate from college. Unfortunately, my parents couldn't sponsor me all the way there, because of how it is in my country. Many people can barely afford to eat. As a result, education has been a secondary issue for most."

"I understand honey. But you don't have to worry about that anymore. You are no longer in the Philippines. You are here now, with me. I will pay all the needed tuition and expenses that will enable you to attend college and graduate to any level of your choice."

"You are a sweet heart," Angie replied.

Tim contacted Columbia University, which is considered one of the best colleges in New York, and Angelina applied for admission, which was approved. Mr. Branch paid the fees required for his wife to attend college and hopefully obtain the education she so much desired. She was scheduled to begin classes the upcoming semester. She wished to major in journalism.

Mr. Branch dropped her off to the house. They kissed each other in front of the building. She walked into the house as Tim stood a little while, watching to make sure she got into the house safely. As she closed the front house door, he waved bye and drove off.

Angelina walked up to her room and went through her student information handbook. She went inside the bedroom, undressed, and put on her usual home clothing. She then sat down in her favorite recliner seat. She picked up the remote control and turned on the television set, then scrolled through the channels until she found her favorite game show. She sat and watched the television show with enthusiasm. She smiled beautifully, stretching her legs straight on the recliner, and her head rested on top of the recliner end. Suddenly, the phone rang. Angelina picked up the phone and said, "Hello!"

"Hello!" the caller replied. "Angelina, this is your aunt Lisa".

"Hi, Lisa".

"I'm here with a friend of mine. As I promised you earlier, I was going to call you back, but yesterday, I was so busy at work. As a result, I couldn't get back to you as quickly."

"Not a problem, I understand".

Lisa intended to visit her niece, so she wanted to know where she was staying. "What is your address?"

"Hold on a second," Angelina replied.

"I wrote it down on a piece of paper. It's in my handbag. Just a second."

She walked quickly into her bedroom and took out her handbag. She removed her note book. "My address is 5555 West Side Street. Do you know how to get here? My husband gave me the direction on how to get here yesterday in anticipation of your call."

"Great. I think I have an idea where you are. Nevertheless, my vehicle is equipped with a navigation system, which can guide me straight to your location."

"Terrific. I'm looking forward to seeing you soon". Lisa immediately began entering the address on her vehicle GPS. She was about an hour away from her location as the GPS indicated.

"OK Angie, we are on our way there. It will be about one hour before we get there, depending on the traffic. We'll see you soon."

"OK. See you then." They hung up.

Lisa and her friend Kikwana began driving slowly in accordance with the city's speed limit toward Angelina's home. They tuned in the radio and was listening to the music as they conversed happily. Angelina went around the house in a hurry, in anticipation of their quick arrival, putting everything in the house in order. Before her guests arrived, the house looked properly dressed and clean. She looked around the house and everything seemed alright to her. She jumped up and down in the living room, and on occasion, peeped through the window to check if her guests have arrived.

Suddenly, the house phone rang. Angelina picked up the phone. She thought it was Lisa. She answered it and heard a man's voice. It was Mr. Branch, her husband.

"Hello dear, how are you doing?"

"I'm fine, just watching television. Lisa and her friend are coming over to see me."

"Lisa?"

"Yes. My aunt Lisa and her friends".

"Uh great. Do they know how to get there?"

"I gave them the address. She has no need for direction from me. She has a GPS navigation system in her vehicle".

"That's wonderful. I hope you'll entertain them very well. You know where everything in the house is now. You all can have a good time. I just called as usual to check up on you. Extend my sincere greetings to your friends".

"I will".

"I'll see you soon. Miss you".

"See you soon." They hung up.

Mr. Branch was getting ready to go for lunch. He began walking out of his office toward the receptionist with a grim smile on his face. Tim rarely smiles grimly. He usually laughs out loud. Monica, Mr. Branch's secretary, noticed the grim smile on his face as he was getting ready to go out for lunch and said, "Hello Mr. Tim, what's that smile on your face? You must have spoken to someone very special. What makes you so happy today?".

Monica was in her fifties. She's been married and divorced and has quite some experience about marriage.

"Yes Monica, you are right. I just finished talking to my lovely wife. My whole life changed for the better since we began living together. She is really a virtuous woman".

"Uh great. No wonder you smile so beautifully. Congratulations. I'm delighted to see you happy and hope it continues this way".

"I hope so myself. I'll be back in one hour. If anyone comes to see me, let them know. I'm out for lunch; and please take good care of them as I would".

"We'll do," Monica said, as Mr. Branch walked out of the office well on his way to lunch.

Lisa arrived at Angelina's house and called her from her cell phone.

"Hello Angelina," Lisa spoke into the phone.

"Hello Lisa."

"We are in front of your house now."

"Okay. You can park there, in front of the yard. I am coming down now to let you in".

"Thank you."

Angelina walked down the stairs to receive Lisa and her friend Kikwana. This was the first time they set eyes on each other after so many years of distance.

"Lisa! Lisa!" Angelina yelled with joy.

Lisa was so happy and said, "Angelina... is this you?"

They both extended their hands and hugged and kissed each other as Kikwana stood and watched with some excitement. "Come on in, fellows". Angelina invited them in to the house and they walked upstairs together, following her.

"Have a seat anywhere you want and make yourselves comfortable".

"Thanks," they said. They sat down close to each other, relaxed and excited.

"What shall I offer you to drink?" Angelina asked.

Lisa and Kikwana stared gently at each other. "We would love rum, beer and sodas of any sort for the mix" said Lisa. She requested a glass of wine with some ice in it, while Kikwana wanted some brandy mixed with ice and soda. Their choices displayed their apparent love for alcoholic beverages; they were ready to have some fun.

Angie immediately went to the bar behind the living room, mixed the brandy with ice and soda and handed the drink to Kikwana. She took a sip and put it down on the table. Angie then went back and brought a bottle of unopened red wine, put it on the table, and brought the ice on a separate plate. Lisa opened the wine first, then put the ice in the cup and poured it into a glass. Angie got herself a bottle of beer. They stood up together, toasted, and were ready to have fun.

Kikwana and Angelina sat down, while Lisa was still standing. She said, "Let me introduce you to Kikwana. Angie, this is Kikwana; Kikwana, this is Angelina, but we call her Angie."

The two women shook hands and exchanged pleasantries.

"Can you turn the music down a little bit?" Lisa continued.

"Oh sure," said Angelina, as she began to lower down the volume from the remote control. Angelina loved loud music. She was very excited to be in the United States. Lisa continued.

"Kikwana is a very good friend of mine. We met each other at work. She is also from the Philippines. She was previously married, but is now divorced. Her ex-husband was very rich, but was a miser. She has two children with him who currently live with her. I'm glad she now lives by herself because she's better off today than when they were together. She currently works with me at the bank as a teller. I'm sure the two of you can make good friends."

"Uh, yeah, that's great. I'm sure we can be good friends. As a matter of fact, we could be like a family". She stood up and went closer to Kikwana and they hugged each other.

"When I first came to the United States, life was so difficult for me. At that time, I couldn't work, because I was ineligible for employment due to the fact that I didn't have a work authorization card from the Immigration and Naturalization service. No one would hire me. I struggled so badly to obtain my work documentation. But that's a total different story that I will not get into right now. I finally got my work authorization card and became employed at a nursing home."

Lisa was so excited to see Angelina that she did not waste much time telling her all of her past issues with employment. Angelina herself was still new to the country and did not know what work authorization meant, but she listened with a lot of interest. Kikwana sat very relaxed. She is aware of all of Lisa's past issues. After all, they have been good friends for many years.

"How do you like America?" Kikwana asked Angelina.

"I love America. I truly love America. God bless America. You know how bad it is in the Philippines. I don't have to tell you. Bad politics, bad leaders, poor economy, crime and corruption. I am happy to be here today. I'm just concerned now about my sister and my mother."

"I am sure that your sister and your mother are very happy that you are here. After all, your husband is rich and you can send money to them every now and then to help them over there. Maybe someday, when you become a citizen, you can bring them over here, but your mother's old age might not permit her to travel outside of the country," Lisa said, adding to the conversation.

"That is one thing I definitely have to do. As you know, I just got here one week ago, but I hope to get my husband on that as quickly. I am sure he will do that. I cook for him and do every other household chore in the house, and I know he loves me. He is a good and kind-hearted man and will do anything for me," Angelina replied.

"Yes, he will. I'm sure he will. Look at all the money he has. He will never spend it all in all his lifetime.

Congratulations. If you ever need us, we are here to help. Just let us know", Lisa said.

"Thanks Lisa, and thank you Kikwana. It is really a pleasure meeting you. I'm happy to get to know you. You have my number and address. Let's keep in touch with each other," Angelina said.

"Oh sure. It's getting a little late now, and we have to get ready to leave, but we'll keep in touch," said Lisa. They bid each other goodbye.

Four.

Tim was done for the day. He was getting ready to go home. He actually finished a little earlier than he was supposed to.

"Monica!"

"Yes, Mr. Branch?"

"I have to go home early today. I need to make several stops to pick up a few items for the house. My wife loves ice cream and the only ice cream shop around our neighborhood is about one mile away. I'll begin heading that direction right now. Please take care of everything."

"No problem, Mr. Branch. I'll take care of things as usual. Take care of yourself".

Tim left his job and headed down the direction of the ice cream store. He got there just in time before the closing hour. He purchased two chocolate ice creams and went to the other store nearby where he usually bought groceries. He bought everything he knew they needed for the night.

He drove home, and when he arrived, he found the yard clean as always. Needless to say, he was very pleased with his wife. He buzzed the door bell and she opened the door. Mr. Branch walked inside as Angelina welcomed him.

"Honey, guess what I got?"

"What?" Angelina asked.

"Ice cream!"

Angelina was so happy to hear that. She loves ice cream. She kissed Tim on the cheek and immediately started licking the ice cream. After a little lick, she gave her husband a kiss in the mouth. They were both happy and enjoying each other.

Angelina began preparing dinner for the night while Tim undressed for the evening. After dinner, they went to bed for the night, having accomplished everything necessary for the day.

The house phone rang and Tim picked it up.

"Hello?" Tim spoke into the phone.

"'Hello, son."

"Hi mom! How are you?"

"All is well, son. I just called to check on you. How is your wife doing?"

"She's fine. I'm beginning to adjust to family life. I never knew how enjoyable family life could be until I married Angelina. She is a wonderful person."

"Good luck to you, son. I'm driving and hope to visit the two of you soon. I'll inform you when it's about time," Victoria replied.

"Thanks mom. I'm looking forward to seeing you."

After Tim hung up, Angelina told him about meeting her aunt last night.

"Honey," my aunt Lisa and her friend Kikwana were here last night. We had a really good time together. Kikwana is a very beautiful young woman and I hope to keep her as a family friend. We talked about a lot of things from the past. She is from the western part of Philippines. Not too far from my home. I enjoyed their company."

"I am glad you are having a good time and keeping good company; that's what life is all about – love, joy, happiness and prosperity. I am taking this week off from work. I intend to take you on a tour around the city so you can get to know some places, so whenever I am not around, you'll be able to get around on your own. This is a great city. I think you should know your way around."

"That's great, honey. You are so sweet."

The next day, Angelina and Tim began dressing up. Tim got ready first and waited patiently for his wife in the living room. He was watching the news while Angelina was still putting on her makeup. She has so many make-up kits. She looked at herself in the mirror but did not think she looked cute enough. She wiped it off and applied a new one.

She finally got ready and they were on their way out to the city for a week-long sightseeing tour. Tim and his wife went all around the city to every known club and hotel of their choice, arena, movie theatres, malls, restaurants and bars. In all, they left nothing untouched. They visited every exciting place they wanted to and knew of.

During their tour, Angelina bought different pairs of shoes, clothes, cosmetics, and hygiene products. She was a lavish shopper and spent quite lavishly. Tim didn't have any problem paying for anything she wanted and purchased, except for things he felt was not needed; he objected to those. Angelina was never happy whenever Tim told her it was unnecessary to spend unwisely, especially on things that were not important or needed. Nevertheless, Tim was able to comfort and console her but not without purchasing those items he objected to.

Angelina and Tim returned home after one week of tour and shopping spree.

"Honey, how did you enjoy the trip?"

"Exciting. I had a really good time," Tim replied.

"Maybe we should do this very often."

"Yes, quite often. Whenever I take time off the job, I lose a lot, but I can easily and quickly make it up."

"Honey, are you saying I'm not worth all the trip?"

"You are worth everything to me. You totally changed me and brought meaning to my life. I only speak in general terms about the state of the economy."

"Okay, honey. You are everything to me too."

They kissed each other, this time subtly, with not much excitement from Angelina. Tim went to bed, feeling happy about how the trip went and ended. He would return to work next week. Angelina unpacked their bags and began putting the items in their proper places. When she took out each dress or shoe, she tried it on and walked toward the mirror to check how it fits. If she didn't like any of it, she blew a big sigh and threw it aside and put on a new one.

Suddenly, the house phone rang. Angelina picked up the handset. "Hello?" she asked.

"Hello, Angelina, this is Kikwana."

"Hi Kikwana."

"Hi, Angelina. Since the last time I left, we haven't spoken, so I decided to call today to make sure I have the right number. So, I had misplaced my wallet after I left your house. I was a little intoxicated that day because I was so excited to meet you. I later found that the wallet was under the chair of Lisa's vehicle. It must have fallen in there when Lisa suddenly slammed on the brake in an attempt to avoid collision with an oncoming truck. She inadvertently drove on the wrong side of the road."

Kikwana explained to Angelina what happened on their way back home. Apparently, they were both intoxicated and shouldn't have driven under the influence.

"Wow! That was scary. I'm happy to hear that that you are alright. I hope Lisa is alright too."

"Yes. She's fine."

"I'm happy to hear from you. Let's keep in touch."

"Yes, we've got to keep in touch."

"Bye, now."

"Bye bye Angelina." They both hung up.

Five

Mr. Branch returned to work after a long week of absence. He's got a lot of work to catch up with. It has been a little hectic for Monica alone and the receptionist to keep the office running without Mr. Branch. But they made it.

Mr. Branch operates a consulting firm. He knows his business well, and has established a strong client base over a period of time. He has been in the business for more than twenty-three years. His clients love him and his work. He is gentle, kind, and has the ability to process things on time with all accuracy.

Monica handed over the deposit slips of all banking transactions done while Mr. Branch was on vacation with his wife. He sat in his executive-style office chair inside his private office/conference room and began going through the lists of transactions while Barbara sat opposite him. He gazed through them line after line. Everything seemed to be correct and accurate. They made a gross deposit of $150,000.00 for the week. Mr. Branch was on a sight-seeing trip. He was pleased with their efforts and signed off the ledger books.

"This was a great week. We made quite a lot of money, and I had a great trip. Thanks Monica, for a job well done."

"You are welcome, Mr. Branch."

Monica walked out of Mr. Branch's office to the general office and sat on her desk waiting to attend to customers.

"Monica, can you please give me a list of some of the clients who came to see me while I was away," Mr. Branch said.

"Sure, Mr. Branch, just a minute."

Monica printed out the list of all the individuals who came to see Mr. Branch while he was on vacation. Monica is a good secretary. She keeps good record of the daily office transactions. She records them in a computer for safety and accuracy and for paperwork reduction. She walked out toward Mr. Branch and handed him the list.

"Thank you, Monica."'

"You are welcome, sir. By the way, your good friend Gary Saturday of Homeland Security, who works for the Citizenship and Immigration Service, was here to see you. You'll find his name there on the list I just gave you."

"Thanks, Monica."

Mr. Branch went through the list. Most of them were his regular customers and had been taken care of by his office when he was on vacation. He had no need to call them. Mr. Saturday's visit was marked personal. As a result, he has to call him.

"Monica, give Mr. Saturday a call. Let him know I'm back. I would like to know the purpose of his visit."

"Okay Sir."

Monica called Mr. Saturday.

"Hello?" Mr. Saturday answered.

"Hello, Mr. Saturday, this is Monica. I'm calling from Mr. Tim Branch's office. He would like to speak to you regarding your visit. Do you have a moment?"

"Yes. I can talk now."

"Hold on."

Monica transferred the phone call over to Mr. Branch.

"Hello, Mr. Saturday. Sorry. I was out when you called. I learned that you were here to see me when I was on a vacation. What can I do for you?"

"Welcome back, Mr. Tim. How was your trip?"

"Great. I had a really good time. My wife and I went out sightseeing in and around the city. I enjoyed every minute of it."

"I'm glad to hear that. Hey Tim, I'm thinking of starting a private business of my own, and that was the reason I came looking for you. I'm seeking your expertise. When will be a good time for us to meet?"

"I'll be in the office all day this week from 10.00 a.m. to 3.30 p.m. You can come in any one of the days between those hours. You can also call me two hours ahead to schedule an appointment."

"Now that I have you on the phone, can I come in on Monday at 1.45 p.m. after lunch?"

"That's a good time."

"Okay. I'll see you then, on Monday."

"See you then."

Tim Branch checked his log sheet to make sure he gave him the right appointment, as he never usually made appointments by himself. Monica usually does, but this time, she was caught up unexpectedly. Mr. Saturday, by the way, is his friend. He didn't need to take him around as he would do other clients. Gary Saturday was pleased with the conversation. He will see Mr. Branch on Monday. Whenever they meet each other, it's all excitement. They usually have long conversations. It is more than business.

Mr. Branch's office phone rang, and Monica picked up the phone.

"Hello, Tim Branch's office. How may I help you?"

"Can I speak to Mr. Branch?"

"May I ask who is calling please?" Monica usually screens all incoming calls before she transfers prospective clients to Mr. Branch. This is their usual office practice. She likes to know who the caller is first. Perhaps, it is something she can handle by herself without getting to Tim.

"I am Mr. Joseph Bright from the office of contracts and bids."

"Hold on for a moment. I'll see if I can get him on the phone."

Monica placed Mr. Bright on hold and asked Tim if he wanted to speak to him, and Mr. Branch was ready to do so. She transferred the call to Mr. Branch.

"Hello, Mr. Bright."

"Hello, Tim. I'm calling to inform you about the bid you placed with our office regarding the supply of medicines to public hospitals. You are the lowest bidder and have been awarded the contract for a period of one year. This will be a one-year ten-million-dollar contract. The terms and conditions will remain the same as in the original bid. I will send the contract agreement to you today and you will receive it in two days. Please go through the contract carefully, sign where indicated, and return the originals within ten days of receipt in the return envelope provided with the package."

"Thanks, Mr. Bright. I am pleased to know that I am the successful bidder. I will wait for the package, and upon receipt, I will sign them as indicated and return them back to you on time." They hung up.

Tim walked toward Monica.

"Monica!" He called to her loudly.

"Guess what?"

"What?" Monica replied.

"We have just won the bid that you placed months ago."

"Really?" Monica said, with lots of joy and excitement. This newly-won contract will result in an increment in Monica's weekly salary. She has been working for Mr. Branch since the beginning of his business. They are now more like a family. Tim shares all his pain and gain with her, including personal and professional matters.

They closed early for the day. Both Tim and Monica left the office to their respective homes. They couldn't be any happier on this day. A ten-million-dollar contract was there in the making. He spoke subtly to himself, "My wife will be happy when she hears this."

He made home safely on time. As usual, his wife welcomed and treated him like the man he always wished to be.

Six

Tim and Angelina woke up together this morning. Tim turned toward his wife and said, "Good morning honey."

"Good morning, sweet heart," Angelina replied. "What do you have planned today?"

"We need to go to the Department of Motor Vehicles. It is time for you to apply for a learner permit. You can begin to learn driving when you obtain the permit. I'm sure you will be able to move around freely once you start to drive. How does that sound?"

"It sounds good to me honey. I never drove before in my life. Back in the Philippines, my parents are quite poor. They can barely afford anything. Even to buy food sometimes is difficult. Owning a car will be like a dream to them." Angelina was very excited about driving. Hopefully, soon, she can become a driver and will get her own car and/or drive Tim's BMW.

"Alright honey. Why don't we start getting ready so that we can head down there? They close at 3.30 p.m. It is usually a long line there, so we need to get there on time if we want to get out of there fast. I still need to get to work today, no matter what."

"Alright, sweet heart. I'm going to get dressed."

Angelina slowly walked into the bathroom. She undressed and got into the bathtub. She turned on the shower and began bathing. When she had finished taking a bath, she walked toward her dressing room and began to pick out the right outfit for the trip to the DMV. She decided to wear a skirt, a light blouse, and a little make up. It was a hot steamy summer day. Tim quickly went into the bathroom and took a quick shower. He got out very quickly and started getting dressed. He put on a blue suit and was ready to make the move. They both finally got ready, ate their breakfast and headed out of the house to the DMV.

As they drove toward the Department of Motor Vehicles, Tim decided to make a stop at a newsstand. He had to purchase a newspaper. Tim usually buys a newspaper there every morning before going to work. The newsstand attendant knows him very well but never saw him with a woman. He also knows Tim's choice of paper, so he has it ready each time Tim pulls up. Parking is usually tight in that area, so he would run out to hand him the paper and get paid.

"Good morning sir, good morning lady," the newsstand attendant said, handing the paper to him.

"Good morning!" Tim and Angelina replied at the same time. Tim's voice echoed first as Angelina's followed.

"Who is this beautiful lady with you, if I may ask?"

"That's my wife. Oh sorry, I should have introduced her to you first. We are heading down there to the DMV for her permit."

"You got a great-looking young woman there. Congratulations."

"Thanks."

Tim handed him $3.00 for the paper and an extra $1.00 tip as usual.

"Thank you, and good luck."

"Bye now. See you tomorrow." Angelina waved a soft goodbye to the newspaper attendant as they drove away.

When they arrived at the DMV, it was a long line as they expected. Tim escorted his wife to the customer service line and walked back to wait at the seating area. He sat down and began reading through the newspaper. Angelina went into the testing area and sat for the permit test. She took the test and passed. She came out smiling as she walked toward Tim. She showed him the permit and the test result. Tim smiled with joy.

"Congratulations. You passed. Okay let's go to the cashier and pay for the permit."

Tim and Angelina walked toward the cashier.

"Good afternoon fellows. Are you here to make a payment?"

"Yes. Good afternoon," Angelina replied.

"We accept cash, check, credit or debit card. How do you wish to pay for this transaction?"

"With a debit card," Tim said, as he handed over his debit card to the cashier. The cashier took the debit card and swiped it through the credit card reader terminal and waited for approval. Within a few seconds, the transaction was approved.

"Sign your name here, please," Tim signed his name at the dotted line on the bottom of the receipt. The cashier tore off the signature part of the receipt. She kept the part with the original signature and gave back the receipt to Tim.

"Mrs. Branch, here is your temporary permit. You can drive with this for now as long as there is a licensed driver in the vehicle. The original permit with your picture on it will arrive at your address within two to four weeks. If after four weeks you still do not receive it in the mail, please feel free to contact the DMV by visiting the web site or by phone as indicated in this notice. Thanks for using the DMV."

"Thank you."

Tim and Angelina began walking out of the DMV as they held each other's hand toward the parking lot. They got in their vehicle and drove home.

"Honey, can I drive now with this learner permit?"

"No. Not as of yet. It only permits you to drive with a licensed driver in the vehicle. But before that, you must learn to drive."

"When can I start to learn?"

"I will contact a local driving school tomorrow so you can begin your driving lesson."

"Honey, why don't you teach me?" She leaned toward his shoulders as she spoke.

"I wish I could, but I can't, not because I don't want to, but because our vehicle is not properly equipped with the safety mechanisms needed to teach driving. As a beginner, a certified driving school and a licensed instructor will be most suitable for you at this time. As soon as you learn to drive, I will be comfortable to drive with you until become confident. Once licensed, I promise to get you your own car."

"A brand new car for me, honey?"

"Yes, a brand new one."

"Uuuh honey. I love you so much."

"I love you too."

They went quiet for a while as Tim continued to drive. Tim looked at Angelina and asked, "What kind of a car do you like?"

"I love trucks. A friend of mine has a very nice truck. Whenever she is on it, she gets a lot of attention from people. They envy her; so do I. I have always dreamed of owning a truck."

"You don't have to dream anymore. It will soon be a reality, a dream come true. I will contact Mercedes Benz. Mercedes has a lot of new trucks out there now, and they are so beautiful. I'm sure you will like it. It is the perfect truck for a woman."

"Yes, honey. I love Mercedes Benz cars. They are just so beautiful," she smiled.

Seven

Tim was happy when he woke up the next morning. Thus far, his marriage was going well. He was happy in this state. He breathed a good sigh of relief. He was glad his wife would soon start to learn how to drive. Perhaps, in the future, she would not have much need of him driving her around. She'll be more on her own. He intended to look for a good driving school to instruct her.

Something struck his mind and he remembered where he took his driving lessons. He thought that would be a perfect school for his wife. He picked his phone book and sought the telephone number of the school he took his driving lessons from. He found the number. Tim called the number from his cellular phone. The phone rang once, and immediately, a recorded message followed – "The number you have dialed is currently disconnected and is not in service. There is no further information available for this number. Please check the number and dial again."

He hung up and thought for a moment. He thought he had dialed the wrong number. He looked at his phone log once again to verify that the number was correct, and it was the right number. He dialed the number once again; this time, slowly and carefully. He got the same recorded message once again. The number was disconnected.

Tim had taken his driving lessons several years ago. He, therefore, concluded that the business may have been closed. In fact, he was right. They were out of business.

Tim looked around and found a telephone book directory. He searched through the driving school section of the directory and found another number for a driving school nearby. He read their profile in the advertisement section of the listings and found it interesting for they offered all kinds of driving services. They could pick up and drop off their students from their home. Their instructors were properly trained and licensed, clean and professional. The payment process was convenient. Anyone could pay with their credit card over the phone or the internet and schedule and receive an appointment for their lessons. He was attracted by their advertisement, which provided just about everything he was looking for.

Tim conferred with his wife to inform her of the information he got.

"Honey, I found a driving school where you may begin your lessons whenever you wish. Do you want me to schedule an appointment for you?"

"Yes, honey."

"When do you want to begin?"

"Any day, any time after 12.30 p.m. will be fine with me. By that time, you will be at work and I'll be alone, and I will have finished by the time you came home from work. This will give me more time to prepare dinner."

Angelina usually gets up early to prepare breakfast for her husband. Once her husband leaves the house, she retreats back into the bed for a little while before she goes to the living room to watch her regular television shows. This makes the afternoon a good time for driving lessons.

Tim took out his debit card from his wallet. He went back to the computer to schedule the driving lesson for Angelina. He selected the beginner package for her and began filling the application. He completed the application, then scrolled down to the payment section of the page, and entered his debit card information to pay for the transaction. His payment was accepted and that took him to the receipt page. He printed out the receipt and the schedule of lessons and handed the information over to Angelina.

Angelina looked at it and she was pleased with it. Her schedule was Tuesday to Friday, from 1.00 p.m. to 3.00 p.m. It was a two-hour practice each day. The driving instructor would pick her up as scheduled for the lessons. Now Angelina was ready to begin her driving lessons.

"Thanks honey. This is good. I'll begin practicing today."

"That's right, sweet heart. The good thing is the flexibility. If you don't like the lessons or the instructor, we can cancel any time. We will be refunded for the lessons you did not take."

Tim got up, put his clothes on, tied his tie, and left for work. Angelina, in the meantime, continued to watch her television show.

After a while, she looked at her gold watch; it was 12.30 p.m. She quickly got dressed, put on a pair of tight jeans, some makeup, and spiky high-heeled shoes. She looked outside through the living room window to see if her instructor had arrived. She saw a white car parked outside, in front of her house. She looked at her watch once again, it was 12.55 p.m. She still had about five more minutes to get down. She picked up her pink sneakers and quickly put them in her handbag. She was ready to go. She started walking outside toward the front door.

The driving school instructor was sitting on the driver's side of the vehicle, reading a magazine while waiting for his student. Suddenly, he heard a noise. He looked up and saw Angelina closing the door. Her behind faced toward him. She was locking the house door. He knew that was his student, but glared lustfully at her boobs. Her butt was thick and curvy. Her stomach was flat, and her breasts stood out. When she had finished locking the doors, she turned around and began walking out of the building and toward the instructor. The instructor quickly got out of the vehicle and stood waiting, with a little smile on his face.

"Good afternoon, Mrs. Branch."

"Good afternoon sir."

"I'm Brian. I'll be your instructor throughout the course of your lessons."

He extended his hand toward Angelina, and Angelina extended hers toward him. They both shook hands.

"Thank you. I'm glad to have you as my instructor. You are right on time. I love people who keep their promise."

"Okay, Mrs. Branch, you can sit here in the driver's seat."

Angelina went slowly and shyly inside the vehicle and sat down in the driver's seat as instructed. She placed her handbag on the rear seat. Brian walked around the vehicle to the passenger side and got in. Mr. Brian was muscular by nature, his chest rocked up and down; his neck was stiff and hair cut short. He was strongly built. As they both sat down, Brian was ready to begin the instruction.

"The first thing you need to know are the basic parts of the vehicle and their functions. Here is the horn, press it." Angelina pressed the horn and it made a very loud sound. Taken by surprise, she yelled, "Oh! Oh!"

"Don't worry about it. Every new student starts out in this manner. Now, the short stick-like metal pointing out here, to your right, is the trafficator, used for signalling. Slide it up and down."

Angelina did as she was told. It made a trafficating noise and the trafficator lights blinked on and off on the dashboard.

"This is used to signal your intention whenever you wish to turn right or left and when changing lanes. The switch beneath the steering to your left side is your light switch. It turns the lights on either high or low beam. It makes the road visible at nights. Pull it."

Angelina pulled the light switch and the lights came on. She pushed it down and the headlights turned off.

"This mirror attached to the glass is called the rearview mirror and can be adjusted accordingly." She looked at the mirror and grabbed it by her right hand and adjusted it properly.

"It looks better now. I can see what's behind without having to look back."

"All right. The mirrors on the left and right sides are called the side-view mirrors. The adjustments can be made by using this button here by your left-hand door". She looked at it and made the proper adjustments.

"The pedals are by your feet. This one is the brake pedal, and this is the accelerator pedal. The accelerator pedal moves the vehicle, while the brake pedal stops the vehicle, when applied. Although there are two pedals, you need to use only one foot, the right foot, to operate both pedals. This handle on the right side of the steering is the gear."

She touched it warmly and nodded her head.

"All right, Mrs. Branch. I'm convinced that you are now familiar with the various parts of a vehicle and it's function. You can also ask me any question, if there is anything you would like me to emphasize more on. I'll be glad to go over it again."

"I understood almost everything, but I will if I have to."

"Okay, let's get started. Place your foot on the break and pull down the gear to the driving position."

She placed her foot on the brake and turned the ignition switch on. When the engine started, she put the gear on the D position. She appeared a little nervous and Brian could sense that. He had to make her feel a little comfortable. He was good at what he did.

"You seem a little nervous. That's not unusual with any new learner. But don't be. You are a beautiful woman. I'm here to assist you. That's my job."

He calmed her down with some sweet words. The word "beautiful woman" really got Angelina started. She burst out into a laughter, looking up, almost forgetting she was learning to drive.

"Thank you," she said, looking back at Brian.

"You can now take your foot off the brake and place it gently on the accelerator." She removed her feet from the brake and placed it on the accelerator. The car quickly moved away from the house with sudden speed.

"Oh... oh..." She screamed.

"Don't panic!" Brian responded, as he quickly applied the safety brake on his side and placed one of his hands on the steering rod.

"I don't think I can do this."

"Yes, you can. You are a learner, and that's what I'm here for, to teach and assist; and that's why there is a safety brake."

"Thanks. Just wait a minute. I think I have to remove my shoes and put on my snickers. I think I can feel more comfortable that way."

"I wanted to tell you about that, but I wasn't sure how you will feel about it. But that will be the best thing to do. For a beginner, you need to be as comfortable as necessary."

Angelina reached back in her hand bag at the rear seat to get her shoes. She placed the handbag on her lap, opened it, and took out a pair of snickers.

"I have to step outside the vehicle for a little while to replace my shoes."

"You don't have to do all that. Stay exactly where you are. I'll help with that."

Brian got out of the car and walked around to the driver's side where Angelina was sitting. He opened the door, knelt, and reached toward her legs while she lifted up her heel. Brian slowly and gently removed the spiky high heels from her legs. He untied the pink sneaker and put it on her foot. He took the other shoe from her left leg, untied it, and put it on her left leg. He handed the pair of the high-heeled shoe back to her and she put it back in her handbag, then threw the handbag over to the rear seat.

"Thanks Brian. You are such a gentleman."

"You are welcome, Mrs. Branch."

"You can call me Angie instead of Ms. Branch."

"Sorry, Angie. My fault. I should have asked you earlier if I should call you by your first name or the last name."

"That's okay."

Angelina was getting ready to get back into the driving practice. She placed her foot on the brake, while the vehicle was still idling, shifted the gear to the driver's position and switched the foot back on the accelerator pedal and drove out slowly. Brian sat and monitored her progress.

"You're doing great. Continue on this side for a while. I'll let you know what to do next. It appears that the sneaker is much more comfortable. It really makes a big difference."

"It was the shoe after all," Angelina said, as they slowly continued driving back on the road. She drove back and forth on the road, stopping perfectly at stop signs and observing every road traffic signs as directed by Brian.

Brian looked at his wrist watch. They had been driving for more than one and a half hour now. They were in an area about thirty minutes away from Angelina's house. Brian decided to teach her how to make a U-turn.

"Angie, when you get to that point right there, you'll have to make a U-turn, and we'll be heading back, on the opposite direction. We have been practicing for a little over an hour and a half now and have thirty more minutes left. That may be enough time to go home, ending your lessons for the day."

"All right, Brian. That's good, because I have to be home early to make ready dinner for my husband before he returns."

Brian did not know that Mrs. Branch was married. He looked right at her and asked.

"Are you married?"

"Yes. My husband is the one who made this lesson possible, but he's at work now. He works Monday to Friday. I'm the only one home when he's at work, that's why you didn't see him when you came to pick me up for the lesson."

Brian was glad to hear this. He perceived himself to be single even though he had two girlfriends, neither of whom knew the other. He could not maintain a steady relationship, because he was always on and off employment.

"Lonely"" he asked curiously.

"Alone. I do nothing else but watch television. I'm home alone, yea, and sometimes lonely."

"Well, you are the only student I have during these hours. After this, my boss lets me off. I'll be free to go home. My mom and I reside together. I hate being there all the time… Hey, if you ever need company, I'm available."

"Well, you are my instructor and I still have many lessons to take. I guess we'll be seeing each other just about every day."

They had arrived home by now, in front of her house. She successfully parked the car. Brian paused for a while.

"My boss is a nut sometimes. He fires and hires people at random. I don't know how long he'll have me there. I may be booted off any time. But take my number, you can reach me anytime"

"You are a really good teacher. I'd rather have you as my instructor than anybody else."

"Make sure you save my number somewhere, just in case I get fired. I'm available any time you need me. I'd love to teach you and keep you company."

"Thank you."

Angelina noted his number on her phone book and got out of the vehicle. Brian got out of the vehicle as well and walked around it toward her.

"Thanks for the lesson."

"You're welcome. Remember to call if you need me for anything. Don't hesitate."

"I will."

They shook hands. She began walking back to the house, while Brian stood and watched until she got inside.

Eight

Tim returned home from work. He had a long busy day at work but was able to deal with it. Tim was always relaxed at home after work. His wife was always there to comfort him.

"Honey, how was the lesson?"

"Great, honey. I had a really good time. I was nervous at first, when I sat on the driver's seat. Remember honey, this is my first time steering."

"Every driver starts out that way. I remember my first day learning to drive. I was very nervous and anxious."

"Really? The funniest part was when the instructor told me to put my foot gently on the accelerator and proceed slowly. I placed my foot on the accelerator pedal and pressed it down hard, and made the car move at a fast speed."

Tim laughed out loud. Angelina continued.

"The instructor quickly applied the safety brakes on his side, causing the car to come to a stop, and then we proceeded normally."

"Uhh... great! How was the instructor?"

"He was really good; he was professional and well-mannered. He knew his job well. I started to get discouraged at first, but he encouraged me."

"Huh? That is a very good thing. I am glad to hear that. Overall, how would you rate him?"

"I'll give him an A."

"Good. I'm glad that it worked out and that you're satisfied with the school."

"Yes, very satisfied. I'll keep working with them until I become a driver, unless something else happens."

"Great. I'm happy this is going the way we wanted it. Honey, I just thought about something."

"What?" Angelina said.

"Now that you are currently unemployed, will you like to work together with me?"

"Umm… Not yet. I'm just comfortable staying at home. I'm not ready to take a job yet. I prefer housework than an office job. The house is clean, your clothes laundered, and meals ready each time you come back from work. Aren't you happy with the way things are right now?"

"I feel good about it. I'm just asking. I don't know how you feel staying home alone when I'm at work."

"I feel pretty good about it. I've worked all my life and I feel like I need a break for a change. You remembered how we first met?"

"At work, right?"

"There you go."

They both laughed till Angie fell backward on Tim's lap. Tim bent over, held her head carefully, and kissed her.

"All right, honey. Here's what I'll do next. Since you have chosen not to work at this time, I'll set aside $1000.00 each week for your personal expense. This is not a salary but a weekly allowance that will enable you to get around and purchase things as needed. You won't have to ask me for money each time you need something, unless that is not enough. How's that?"

"That is a great idea, honey. I thought about that myself, but I didn't want to ask because I know you have a lot of things to take care of."

"Well, you are my wife, and you shouldn't hesitate to ask me for anything."

Tim reached inside his wallet and pulled out $1,000.00 in clean cash and gave it to her. She took the money from him, looked at it, but did not count it; she threw it aside on the table. Every week, she began to receive her weekly $1000.00 allowance from Tim.

As both of them laid beside each other, Angelina suddenly began rubbing her stomach, moaning quietly in pain. Tim got right up and started asking her questions.

"What's the matter honey? Honey, what's the matter?"

"My stomach."

"Your stomach? What about your stomach?"

"Uh, Uh, Yes. My stomach. it's hurting very bad."

Tim got up, went to the wardrobe, picked up his clothes, and began putting them on.

"We got to go to the hospital right away," Tim said, as he was still getting dressed. He picked up the house phone and dialed his doctor. The phone rang twice and the receptionist picked up.

"Hello, Doctor Emelie's office. How can I help you?"

"Good afternoon. This is Tim Branch. My wife has a serious stomach pain and we would like to come over to see you."

"Okay, Mr. Branch, the doctor is here and you can come in any time before 8.00 p.m."

"Thank you, we are on our way."

Tim hung up. He held Angelina by the hand and walked downstairs to the vehicle and drove off to the clinic, which was about one mile away from their home, so it did not take them long to get there.

They arrived at the clinic in about 15 minutes and walked up to the doctor's office. The receptionist welcomed them.

"Welcome. How may I assist you?" said the receptionist.

"My stomach just began hurting very badly this morning."

"Are you still experiencing such pain right now?"

"Yes, but mildly."

The receptionist gave her a sign-in and a valuation sheet. She signed and completed the evaluation sheet and gave back the papers to the receptionist.

"Thank you. You can have a seat. The doctor will be with you shortly."

Mr. Branch and Angelina sat down in the waiting area, waiting to be called. The receptionist walked in to the doctor's room and gave the evaluation sheet to the doctor. He took a brief glance at it."

"Okay, you can send them in," the doctor said. She walked out toward the couple to see them.

"Mrs. Branch, come with me. The doctor is ready to see you."

Angelina walked toward the back door to meet the doctor, while Tim sat in the waiting area. He was reading a magazine. Tim took his cell phone out of his pocket and called his office. Monica answered the call. She knew that was her boss Tim calling through the caller identification.

"Hello Tim," Monica said.

"Hey! I'll be running late to work today. I'm not even very sure if I can make it there. I'm at the clinic with my wife and I'm not sure when we will leave here."

"Is everybody okay?

"She complained of having stomach pain and cramps earlier this morning. We are here and she is with the doctor as we speak. If anyone there for me, let them know that I may not make it to work today. They can try another day."

"Okay sir. I'm sure she will be fine. I remember when I first got pregnant. I was in a lot of pain, not knowing what it was, until we came to the hospital. But I got your message and will do as you have instructed."

"Thank you," Tim hung up.

"Mrs. Branch, I'm a doctor, Patrick Emelie. I went through your profile and realized that you have some pain in the stomach."

"Yes doctor."

"On the right side?"

"When did this start?"

"Early in the morning."

"Please lay backward here."

She laid down on her back. Doctor Emelie began pressing his hands on her stomach.

"Do you feel anything?"

"No."

After about thirty seconds, he checked her heartbeat.

"Your heartbeat is normal. I don't see anything wrong. Everything seems to be normal. But I need to conduct some additional tests. Do you have children?"

"No."

"So you have never been pregnant in the past?"

"No."

"Well, it sounds like pregnancy to me, but just to be sure, I will have to run a pregnant test. Do you wish to do that?"

"Yes."

Doctor Emelie drew some of her blood and walked out to the testing room to conduct a pregnancy test. The test result was positive. He walked back to the checkup room where Angelina was sitting.

"Mrs. Branch, the results are here. Just as I thought, it came out to be positive. This means you are pregnant." Angelina smiled.

She got up and walked out toward the waiting area. Tim sat there waiting. He had nodded off. Angelina poked him.

"Honey, we can leave now. We are finished" She was ecstatic.

"How did it go?"

"Everything went well. It wasn't what we thought. It's pregnancy."

Tim smiled joyfully. He hugged and kissed her. They got into the vehicle and drove straight home.

Tim was so happy to hear this. He was unaware of signs of pregnancy. His wife was already one-month pregnant. With joy and excitement, he picked up the phone and dialed his mother. The phone rang and his mother answered.

"Hello, son?"

"'Hello Mom. I got some good news today."'

"'Tell me about it."

"My wife is pregnant."

"Really?"

"Yes. We are just coming back from the hospital. She was complaining of stomach pain early this morning, but we weren't sure what it was. Then, we decided to go to the clinic to see the doctor. After several check-ups, the doctor ran a series of tests intended to identify the cause of the pain. In the end, we found that she is pregnant."

"Congratulations. That is how pregnancy works in the early stages. She'll start having some morning sickness. That reminds me of my pregnancy of you. I experienced the same thing. Your dad took me to the doctor. That was how I discovered that I was pregnant."

Tim's mom had several children. She knew exactly what she was saying.

"Now son, you take good care of your wife from now as you always do till she delivers. Do as much to avoid any arguments with her. Most pregnant women are usually irritated."'

"'Thanks mom. I'll do just as you have told me."

"'Good luck to the both of you."'

Eight months later, Angelina had a baby boy, and they named him Tim Branch Jr.

Nine

Tim and Angelina loved their new son dearly. This was the best thing to have ever happened to them. Tim made a very good father. He loved to spend time with his son. He took time off his job as often as needed to help in the upbringing of his son Tim Jr. He was playing with his son in the living room when the doorbell rang.

Tim quickly ran to the door to see who it was. It was the mailman.

"Good afternoon sir," the mail carrier said.

"Good afternoon," Tim replied, as the mailman handed over to him some mails. He quickly flipped through them. There was one that came from the Immigration and Naturalization service, from the Department of Homeland security. Inside it was a green card, also known as an Alien Registration Card. His wife Angelina was finally granted the permanent resident status of the United States of America. Tim was so happy to see that. He went back into the house with the mails.

"Angie?"

"Yes honey?"

"I just received your green card. You have been granted the status of a permanent resident of the United States of America as expected."

Angelina took the green card from Tim and looked at it. The picture looked pretty good to her. She screamed in delight.

"Yeah. It's finally here. Does that mean that now I'm an American?"

"Yes. Now, you can also become a citizen."

A permanent resident status is usually granted to the spouse of a United States citizen. Tim had applied to the Immigration for his wife to obtain the permanent resident status by marriage.

The time was fast approaching and Tim was ready to go to work. He got ready and went off to work as usual, while Angelina stayed home with their son watching television. After a little while, she dialed her friend Kikwana. The phone rang and Kikwana picked up.

"Hello Angie?"

"'Hello Kikwana."

"How are you doing?"

"I'm fine."

"How about the baby?"

"He's doing pretty fine. He's here lying down beside me. His father has just left for work. But guess what?"

"What?"

"I just got my green card"'

"Congratulations."

"Thank you. My husband just received the mail. He opened it and there was the card. He came and gave it to me, played a little with his son, and left for work."

"Oh good. I'm happy that it is finally here. You got it right on time. It usually takes about this long. You are now on your way to becoming an American citizen. Do you know what that means?"

"No. Tell me about it."

"That means you now have the same rights as your husband. You don't have to be home anymore, washing dishes and cooking for him as if you were a house maid. You can do anything you want now."

"Really?"

"Yes, for real."

"I've waited a long time for this day to come. I have always wanted to visit my country, but couldn't, because I was waiting for this to be approved."

"Well, you don't have to wait any more, because now you can travel back and forth as you wish, without needing a visa."

"Yea? That visa thing is a headache."

"You're right. It usually takes a process. I will have to call you soon again. We gotta get out and celebrate."

"I'm ready when you are."

They hung up. Angelina was so excited about the whole thing. She had one more person to inform about this good news. She picked up the phone again and dialed her aunt Lisa. The phone rang and Lisa picked up.

"Hello Angie"

"Hello Lisa. How are you doing?"

"I'm doing great. How about you?"

"I'm fine. I've got some good news for you."

"Yea."

"Yeah, I got my green card."

"Congratulations. That was quick."

"Yes. It came very fast. I just spoke to Kikwana, and she said the same thing."

"Yea. Kikwana was right. Some people usually have to wait a long time before they get it. You are just lucky."'

"Yes, I guess I am. I just had a baby. My husband bought a car for me and now my green card is here as well."

"Well, you can say that your baby brought you good luck. Now that you have your green card, you can enjoy all the benefits an American can avail, and that includes freedom."

Kikwana was glad to hear that. In her country, people were not really free. Women don't have all the rights as men.

"Yes. Freedom is the most important thing to me. You know how it is in the Philippines. Women don't have that much freedom."

"Congratulations. I guess one day, if you have time, we can go out and have some drinks."

"Yes. I have all the time in the world. We'll talk later."

"Bye for now."

"Bye." They hung up.

Angelina immediately started singing and dancing and clapping in front of her boy. After a while, the doorbell rang. She paused and walked toward the door. It was her husband. She opened the door and let him in.

"Welcome honey." She hugged and kissed him. Tim walked inside and walked upstairs to his room. He undressed and put on his evening pajamas. He walked toward the baby, picked him up, and began playing with him as usual. Angelina walked toward him.

"How was your day?"

"Pretty hectic. I was extraordinarily busy today."

"You mean to tell me you had a bad day?"

"Not like a bad day. Just hectic."

"You're pretty used to it. What made this day so hectic and different from other days?"

Angelina never ran a business. She didn't understand what business pressure meant. She thought it was just like a regular day job.

"It wasn't any different than the other days, but there are days that are just more hectic than other days. I had a tough client, whose work we couldn't finish as promised. He was pretty angry about that. He got into a little verbal match with Monica. I had to get involved at a point to help stabilize things. I managed to convince him and guaranteed him that his job will be completed by tomorrow, no later than 4.00 p.m."

"That's great. So, were you able to convince him?"

"Yes, I was."

"So the day ended well then"

"Sort of. It ended quite well."

It was getting close to 7.30 p.m. Tim and Angelina usually had their dinner at 8.30 p.m. Tim was getting a little hungry; he couldn't help but ask his wife about dinner.

"What are we having tonight for dinner?"

"Honey, uh, today I wasn't able to cook anything. I was so happy about the green card. I was busy talking to Lisa and Kikwana. They were happy to hear the news. After talking to them, I took a bottle of red wine you left over last night and drank whatever was left. After that, I dosed off. By the time I got up, I was so tired that I wasn't able to cook anything."

"I'm sure you would be tired. I'm happy that you are happy. My job is to make you happy. I'll be going over to the fast food restaurant over there to grab something for us."

"What do want for yourself?"'

"Get me a milk shake, a hamburger, and large fries."

"Okay. I'll be back."

Tim got up and started getting ready to go to restaurant. He put on his blue jeans, a light sweatshirt, and sneakers.

"Do you wanna go with me?" Tim asked.

"No, honey. I'm too tired. I'll wait till you get back."

Tim went out and drove to the restaurant around the corner from their house. It was raining very heavily that night. Tim was not used to driving at night, especially in the rain. He had second thoughts about driving in the rain, but being quite hungry, he wanted to eat as well as satisfy his wife. He got to the restaurant, but it was closed for the night. It wasn't a twenty-four-hour operation.

"Oh shit! They are closed," Tim yelled out with disappointment. He became a little frustrated. He reached for his phone and called his wife. Angelina answered.

"Hello?"

"Honey, they are closed."

"Is that the only restaurant around the area?"

"No. But I'm not sure of another one nearby."

"Why don't you call the information line and ask?"

"Oh yes, that's a good idea. I'll do that."

Tim hung up. He wanted to call the info line and find out, but he remembered another restaurant somewhere midtown. He slowly made a U-turn and proceeded toward that direction. Tim was fortunate this time; the restaurant was open. He drove by the drive through and placed two orders of milk shake, hamburgers and large fries. He paid the cashier, picked up the order, and started driving home slowly.

When he got home, he was greeted warmly by his wife.

"What took you so long?" Angelina asked.

"The next store I found was too far away, but I had to go there anyway."

"I was starving to death waiting for these fries."

She took the meal, opened the box, and removed hers. They ate heartily and then called it a night.

Ten

Mr. Branch woke up the next morning after a good night's sleep. Angelina was still sleeping. He did not want to disturb her by waking her up. He got up and went to the bathroom. He brushed his teeth and took a quick bath. He had been going to work very late recently due to his desire to meet his wife's needs, but he was now determined to be at work on time every day, in order to avoid losing most of his clients.

After he got dressed for work and began walking to the door, Angelina heard him and woke up. She got off the bed sluggishly.

"Honey, is that you?"

"Yes baby."

"Are you on your way to work?"

"Yes. I woke up early, but didn't want to wake you up. You were deep asleep. I felt you were perhaps dreaming."

"No, I was just tired. I'm usually slow waking up in the morning, as you already know. Come and give me a kiss before you leave."

Tim walked back to the bedroom, and as he approached, Angelina got up slowly, and they kissed each other.

"I gotta go now," Tim said.

"Alright, see you when you get back."

Tim walked out and went to work. Angelina got up and looked through the window to make sure Tim had gone far away. She could not see his vehicle. She was now sure he had gone far down. She walked back to the bathroom and washed her mouth thoroughly. She went back to the kitchen and prepared breakfast for herself. By the time she had finished eating breakfast, the phone rang. Angelina picked up.

"Hello?" she said.

"Hello Angie, this is your mom."

"Hi mom, how are you doing?"

"Fine, but not so good. Your father is sick. He is in the hospital."

"What's wrong with him?"

"He has been feeling cold and has been shivering. As a result, we had to take him to the hospital."

"How long has he been there?"

"He has been there for quite some time now, about one week."

"Really? How is he feeling now?"

"I guess, much better. The doctor said he will be discharged in two days."

"I hope they do not discharge him until he has fully recovered."

"I hope the same as well, and that is the best thing to do. But as you know, it costs a lot to keep someone in the hospital here in the Philippines, and we don't have any money to keep him there. This is the reason the hospital had to discharge him early, so he may continue to recover from home."

"Well, if that is the case, don't worry about it so much. Money will not be an issue. I will send you some money this afternoon to help care for him while he is at home."

"Thank you very much. That will be very helpful to us."

"You will need an identification card to receive the money. Do you have one?"

"Yes."

"Alright. Expect to hear from me soon."

"Okay."

They hung up. Angelina got dressed. She wanted to look for a place to make the transaction. She called a local taxi cab company. The taxi arrived within five minutes. She got into the vehicle and sat in the rear seat.

"Driver."

"Hello ma'am."

"Take me to the nearest Western Union office."

"Yes ma'am."

The driver drove quickly to a nearby Western Union office and pointed to the store, looking at Angelina.

"Wait here for me. This is going to be a round trip. I will not be long."

"Okay, ma'am"

Angelina got out of the vehicle and walked toward the store to make her transaction. She stood in line until it was her turn. She walked to the cashier.

"Hi. I would like to send $5000.00 to the Philippines."

"Okay ma'am, do you have any identification?"

"Yes."

She took out the identification card from her wallet and presented it to the cashier along with the money, which included the cost to send it. The cashier gave her an application to fill out. She quickly filled it out and handed it back to the cashier. The cashier went through the application, and when she was done, she counted the money, processed the transaction, and printed out a receipt.

"Okay. Ma'am, sign your name here by the dotted line."

Angelina took the receipt from the cashier and signed her name where indicated and gave it back to the cashier. The cashier gave back the second part of the receipt for the transaction to Angelina.

"Thanks for choosing Western Union."

"Thank you."

She walked out of the Western Union office and got back into the taxi cab, which was waiting for her outside. She opened the door of the taxi and sat at the back of the vehicle.

"Okay, you can take me back to where you picked me up."

"Okay, ma'am."

The driver put the gear in reverse position, backed up a little bit, made a U-turn, and headed back towards Angelina's residence. They arrived within ten minutes and Angelina was ready to pay for her trip.

"What's the fare?"

"Fifty dollars round trip."

Angelina handed the driver a one-hundred-dollar bill. The driver looked at it. It was a hundred-dollar bill. He began to count as Angelina began to exit the vehicle. He thought she was coming toward his side to pick up the change, but she continued walking toward the front door to her home.

"Ma'am, you forgot your change," the driver said.

"You can keep the change. Thanks for the trip."

"Thank you. Here is our card. You can call us any time you need a taxi."

Angelina took the business card from the driver and left. On entering the house, she looked at the clock. It was about 1.30 p.m. The time in the United States of America differed from that of the Philippines by four hours.

It was about 5.30 p.m. in the evening over there. Angelina thought it was a good time to call her mother. She removed her cell phone from her hand bag and dialed her mother's number in the Philippines. It was cheaper to make an international call from a landline phone than from a cell phone. However, it was more convenient for her to use a cell phone than a landline because of the freedom to move around while talking. Her mother immediately answered the phone at first ring.

"Hello!"

"Hello mom, It's Angie."

"Hi, Angie?"

"I've got some information for you."

"Okay."

"I've just sent $5000.00 to you to help pay dad's hospital bill."

"Thank you, Angelina. Your father will be glad to hear this."

"No problem mom."

"How do I get the money?"

Her mother had never received money from abroad before. Like most foreign countries, they receive money through family members or friends. She thought she would receive the money from someone sent by Angelina.

"Get a pen and paper and I will give you the details."

"Okay. Hold on a minute while I look for a pen."

She ran outside her room and found a pen and a piece of paper. She could not read or write because she was uneducated. She called her daughter who was at home at the time. She had not yet gone out with her boyfriend. They were preparing to.

"Sussanah, come here please. Your sister Angelina is on the phone."

"Okay mom, I'm coming."

Sussanah ran to the living room, took the phone from her mother, and took the pen and the paper from her.

"Hello, Angie?"

"Hello Sussanah."

"Dad is sick and is in the hospital."

"Yes. Mom told me already. Now write this number down."

"Okay. Go ahead."

She called out the tracking number on the Western Union receipt as Sussanah wrote it down.

"Give his number to mom. She can take it to a Western Union location there and pick up the money tomorrow."

"Okay. Thanks Angie. We certainly appreciate it."

They hung up.

Eleven

Tim Branch was ready to leave his office for the day. As usual, he called his wife to make sure she is alright.

"Hello honey, where are you?"

"I'm in the office, but I'm getting ready to come home."

"Alright. On your way home, please stop by the restaurant down the road and pick up something for us for dinner."

"Okay. What do you want for yourself?"

"You can get me a well-done sirloin steak with some rice, corn and collard greens. I think that will be fine for me."

It will be a while before I get home. As you know, the restaurant there is usually busy."

"Take your time. There is no rush."

"Alright, see you in a bit."

"See you soon."

She hung up. Tim left his office, got in the car, and headed down to the restaurant to get some food for the night. He got to the restaurant and parked his vehicle by the roadside. He walked into the restaurant and placed his order. The order was ready faster than Tim expected. The attendant walked toward him with the order.

"Your order is ready," the cashier said.

"How much is it?"

"Seventy-five dollars, sir."

Tim handed her the money for the order and took the food from the cashier.

"Thank you, sir, and have a nice day."

"Thank you."

Tim headed out toward home with the meal. When Tim got home, Angelina immediately rushed to the door.

"Welcome back honey," Angelina said, as she received the meal from him.

"Thanks. How is everybody doing?"

"We are both fine, waiting for you to come home."

Tim went into the bedroom and began to undress. When he had finished taking off his clothes, he wrapped a shower towel around his waist and went to the bathroom. He took a quick bath, came out of the shower and was ready for dinner. After dinner, Angie had something to tell him.

"Honey, I thought about something."

"Tell me."

"We will need a babysitter to help look after our child."

"That's a good idea. But honey, you are not currently working. Why would we need someone to babysit when you are always home?"

"Sometimes, I need to step out of the house for some air."

"And so does the baby. Why won't you take him out with you?"

"It isn't like I don't want to take him with me, but I can't take him with me every time I go outside. That's a little inconvenient for me. Is that what you want?"

"No, that's not what I am saying."

"Then what are you saying?"

"I'm saying that in my opinion, this is not the right time to leave a baby with a sitter so you can step outside."

"A babysitter is not a stranger Tim. She is an employee."

"I understand that, but you are the mother. Some of these nannies can't be trusted, especially when a baby is that young."

"I don't go that far out from the house. I'm always around."

"I'll suggest that for now, you can put him on a baby stroller since you are always around the house. Besides, you told me that you prefer to raise the child by yourself first before anything else."

"Well, my friend Kikwana has a nanny who takes care of her children while she is at work."

"Yes. Your friend Kikwana can have a nanny to take care of her children because she works and is unmarried and fully employed. She needs to have someone who takes care of her kids while at work. Your situation is different."

"Honey, why do we have to go through this? I'm sick and tired of arguing. This argument is unwarranted and simply baseless. I told you I need a babysitter and I need one right away."

"Are you giving me an ultimatum?"

"I don't know what giving you an ultimatum means, but I know that I need one within the next forty-eight hours, by the end of this week."

"Really? First of all, you don't find babysitters just like that. You've got to search for one – a reputable person who you can trust."

"I know of one already."

Tim marveled at all this. He was beginning to retreat from the argument. He suddenly became quite confused with the whole thing.

"How, when and where did you meet her?"

"Kikwana has a friend who just came to the country and is looking for a job. I met her and got to know her the last time I visited her."

"Does she have the authorization to work in the United States? It is against the law to hire someone who is not authorized to work in America. If caught, they can be subjected to financial and criminal punishment."

"Nobody will know that she is illegal while she is with us. I know of many people in America who work without proper documentation."

"I know about that too, but we can't violate the law because someone else did. They just haven't been caught yet."

"This is our business and not someone else's. No one will know what she is doing here for us. They may think she is one of my sisters, and besides, you can pay her by cash."

Tim now realized that he couldn't win this argument. He got tired of talking back and forth with her and didn't want to hurt their relationship. He had given up to her demand. He walked to the bedroom, shut the door, and laid down to sleep.

The following morning, Tim woke up and was ready to go to work. Angelina was still sleeping. He did not want to wake her up. When Angie woke up, she realized that Tim had left for work. She looked pretty sad. This was the first time Tim had left home without saying anything to her. She walked toward the living room, picked up the phone, and called Tim.

"Hello honey," Tim answered.

"When did you leave the house?"

"In the morning, for work."

"Without talking to me?"

"Sorry, you were asleep and I didn't want to disturb you."

"That's crap. You should have woken me up before you went away. You said nothing to me and did not kiss me. You just walked away quietly like that?"

"Sorry honey. That was my fault. I didn't mean to."

Angelina hung up on him. She picked up the phone and called her friend Kikwana. Kikwana answered.

"Hello Angie?"

"Good morning Kikwana."

"Good morning to you."

"Will you be working today?

"No. It's my off today. I feel so tired, I didn't feel like working today, so I called my supervisor to let him know that I will not make it to work today."

"Is he alright with that?"

"Yea. He didn't like the idea, but he had to accept it. I lied to him. I told him I was going to the clinic for a checkup. He believed me but asked me to get him some proof of attendance from the clinic."

"Will you go to the clinic?"

"Hell no!"

"How then will you get him the proof?"

"A friend of mine works at the clinic. I'll ask her to write me a letter to that effect. She can verify my attendance."

"Ha ha ha" Angelina laughed.

"You know your way around, huh!"

"I've been doing this for a long time. I can get away with anything."

"My husband and I got into a heated argument last night."

"About what?"

"About the baby sitter."

"So you told him already?"

"I told him yesterday after you told me that Lissandra is looking for a job."

"What did he say?"

"He nagged about it. He asked why I needed a baby sitter. Could I not take care of my own child?

"Why can't he babysit himself? That's his child too!"

"Don't pay him no mind. He makes thousands of dollars every day and never gives me anything. At the same time, he expects me to sit at home and be a housewife."

"I'm sure he thought he found a slave. He thinks you don't know any better because you are of a foreign background. Perhaps, he will be better off being divorced."

"I'm coming over anyway to your house since you are home today. We can talk more about Lissandra's pay."

"Okay. I'm waiting for you. I know this isn't something we can talk about on the phone."

"I'm on the way."

Twelve

Immediately after talking to Kikwana, Angelina got dressed. She looked appealing and beautiful as always. She dressed her son up, put him on the baby stroller, and pushed the stroller downstairs toward the parked Mercedes Benz. She went to the back of the car, took out the baby car seat and attached it properly to the back of the car seat. She then placed the baby comfortably in the chair and buckled him. She then drove off to the park near the area.

It was a playground. Most people brought their children to that park. They sat on the park and played around there for a while. When she had finished playing in the park for about one hour with the child, they got back into the vehicle and began driving toward Kikwana's residence.

When she arrived at Kikwana's house, she found a place and parked her vehicle. She removed the baby from the car and carried him on her chest and walked into the elevator of the building. Kikwana lived on the fourth floor of the building. She rang the bell and Kikwana let them in.

"Hi, Angie."

"Hello Kikwana."

"So you finally made it here."

"Yes. We had to stop at the playground for a little while."

"Come on in and have a seat anywhere."

Angelina walked to the chair on the opposite side of the room and sat down, Tim Jr. on her lap. Kikwana walked toward Angie and intended to play with the kid.

"Hey cutie! Look at him. So cute."

Angelina sat smiling as Kikwana cheered on and praised her son.

"He looks exactly like his father."

"Yes, he does."

"Would you like anything to eat or drink?"

"It's too hot today. I don't feel like eating anything, but a little soda or something will be good for me."

Kikwana went to her refrigerator and took out a bottle of soda and put it on the table where Angelina was sitting. She opened the bottle and poured a little soda into the glass while Angelina sat beside her.

"Well baby, let's talk", Kikwana said.

"Yes. It's about Lissandra. I remember you told me she is looking for a job."

"Yes. She has been looking for a job for a long time now, but hasn't found one. I guess, and I am sure, it is because she doesn't have the qualifications needed for a job. Additionally, she is not legally authorized to work in the United States yet."

"Don't worry about it. I can be of great help to her. I can hire her just as she is for babysitting Tim. Most babysitters get a minimum wage, but I can offer her a flat weekly salary of $450.00. I am sure that will help her for the start."

"Yes certainly. And it is all cash. She can live comfortably with that. She shares a room with a friend. I am sure she will do better with this job. Perhaps, she can find her own apartment".

"Why don't you give her a call so she can come over and we can discuss her job, duties and salary together."

"OK."

Kikwana called Lissandra. The phone rang and she answered.

"Hello, Kikwana?"

"Hello Lissandra."

"Where are you?"

"I'm home. Sitting here, doing nothing."

"Why don't you come over to my house? My friend Angelina is here with me and would like to discuss a job offer with you."

"Okay. I'm on the way to you now. I'll probably get there in about one hour."

"Okay. See you soon."

Kikwana hung up and turned toward Angelina. Lissandra immediately got dressed and was headed to meet Angelina and Kikwana.

"She is on her way and is expected to be here in about one hour," Kikwana said to Angelina.

"Great. We'll see her soon."

One hour later, Lissandra arrived at Kikwana's residence. She rang the doorbell and Kikwana got up and opened the door for her. She came in and was well received by them.

"Lissandra, this is my good friend Angelina. She is the one I told you was looking for a nanny for her young one."

"Alright. Hi, Ms. Angelina. I'm happy to meet you."

"I'm fine. How about you?

"I would like to say that I'm fine now that I finally met you. Kikwana told me about you and your intentions to hire me as your baby sitter."

"Yes. My son is two years old today," pointing over to her son.

"Oh, that's him right there. Look at him. He's so cute."

"Yes, he is. He resembles his father."

Lissandra praised the little boy as much as she knew how to. That was expected of her after all; that was the baby she would be taking care of. She had to show his mother that she was friendly with kids and was capable of taking care of him.

"Well, getting right to the point, Kikwana told me that you are a very good person, hardworking and good with children."

"Yes. Kikwana is right. I have babysitted for one family in the past. Their kid was very rough. But it takes someone with care and patience to handle children. You can count on me to take good care of your child. No worries."

"That's good to hear. But if I may ask, why did you quit?"

"I didn't actually quit; they couldn't afford to keep me any longer. I was getting paid $250.00 each week, and I

101

had to pay my fare back and forth and buy my own food. Her husband lost his job and they had to pay me off. Ever since then, I have been out of work."

"Where do live currently?"

"I reside with a friend of mine at the moment. I'm supposed to contribute toward the monthly rent, but for the past three months, I haven't been able to make my contribution to the rent. Yet, they are willing to house and feed me until I find something to do."

Angelina was moved by her responses. She felt the need to hire her almost instantly.

"How much salary are you expecting now, should I hire you?"

"Well, I'm hoping to get about four hundred dollars every week, but I'm willing to negotiate."

"Say I decide to hire you today, when can you start?"

"I'm willing and ready to start now."

Kikwana stood silent while Angelina and Lissandra conversed. They were friends for a while and she was a good lady, besides the fact that she was having difficulties. Lissandra told Angelina all about her life and previous employments.

"Well, Lissandra, you don't have to worry much now. I heard all that I wanted to know, and I am very satisfied with what I heard, besides the fact that you were referred to me by Kikwana, a good friend of mine. I will begin by offering you $500.00 per week. I will give you a room in the basement section of the house, well furnished with all amenities, and you do not have to pay rent or buy food. Your job duties are pretty simple, keeping the house clean and taking care of my son when I'm absent, but I'm mostly in the house anyway."

Lissandra smiled happily. She hugged Angelina with tears of joy dripping down her lashes. She put her palms together and looked toward the ceiling, seemingly praying, "Thank you Jesus."

Her long-sought prayers have been answered.

"But there's just one thing I want to make known to you."

"Okay."

"You have to keep your salary a secret. I don't want my husband to know anything about it because he doesn't want me to hire a baby sitter."

"Why?"

"He thinks there is no need for one since I'm not working. Therefore, I should be the wife, mother, and babysitter as well."

"Hmm..."

"Your salary will come straight from me in cash. Do you understand?"

"Yes, of course. I don't know your husband. I know you. Your husband did not hire me. You did."

Kikwana has kept silent enough. She is now ready to join the discussion.

"Did you hear everything she told you?" Kikwana asked.

"Yes. I heard her loud and clear, and will do just as she said."

"Well, Lissandra, I'm letting you know this for real as a friend. The day her husband knows about your salary is the day your job will end. If you wanna keep this job, you better do as she says."

"I will."

Angelina officially hired Lissandra and the latter agreed to babysit for her under her terms and conditions.

It was already late in the evening. Angelina and Lissandra were still in Kikwana's house and it was just about time for Mr. Branch to come home from work. Mr. Branch had called the house phone to inform Angelina that he was getting ready to leave work. Their house phone rang several times, but no one was there to answer it. It went to the voice mail. He then dialed her cell phone. Her phone was in the silent mode, so she didn't realize Tim had called. When she was getting ready to leave, she looked at her cell phone, intending to place a call and saw a missed call from her husband. She called him back and Tim answered.

"Hello honey."

"Hello. Sorry I missed your call."

"I had called the house earlier, but no one answered."

"Yes. I was away. I went to my friend's house with the kid earlier this afternoon, but we are well on our way home now. We should be there within the next thirty minutes."

"OK. Well I'm about to leave work myself. I'm running late today. I have a few more things to do before I exit. I should be home hopefully in the next two hours."

"No worries honey. We'll see you then." They hung up. Angelina turned to Kikwana.

"Well Kikwana, it has been a pleasure to spend time here with you today."

"Likewise. It's always a pleasure to have you."

"It's getting a little late, so I think we should be heading back home now."

Angelina stood up and Lissandra picked up the baby stroller; they walked out of the house and headed home. Lissandra was right at work.

Thirteen

Angelina returned home with her new nanny and housekeeper Lissandra. She opened the door and they walked into the house. Lissandra carried the baby as they walked upstairs. They came up to the living room and Lissandra sat down there while Angelina walked into the bedroom and began to undress. She put on her night gown and walked over to Lissandra in the living room.

"Alright Lissandra, welcome home. Follow me and I will walk you around the house."

Lissandra got up and followed her as she requested. She took her downstairs to the basement of the house. There was the guest room, fully and well furnished. It had a full bath, a dining area, kitchen, living room and bedroom. This was where Angelina intended Lissandra to stay.

"Lissandra, this is your apartment. This is where you will be staying for the time you will be working for me. All these are now yours. The refrigerator is filled with different varieties of food. You can use them as you wish, and whenever it runs out, don't hesitate to inform me. I will refill it.".

Lissandra was so pleased with everything that her newfound job had to offer. She was delighted to be there. Most of the things she lacked had now become available to her.

"Thanks Angelina. I'm happy to be here and am happy to be a part of your household."

She couldn't stop thanking Angelina. She was so joyful. She now lived in a big house with her own television, bed and bathroom, without having to share with anyone. Most importantly, she might never have to pay rent for the period of her employment with this family. She thanked Angelina again for her kindness and got straight to work.

Tim returned home in a while. He rang the doorbell. Lissandra ran to the door. She saw a man standing in front of the door. Having not met Tim before, she opened the door to know who the man was looking for.

"Hello," she said, holding the door halfway open as Tim was about to walk in.

"Hello?" Tim said, looking at her with astonishment.

"Hello sir. Welcome."

"Thank you?", Tim replied, walking upstairs. At first, he thought Lissandra was Angelina's friend.

"Angie?"

"Yes honey. I'm in the shower. I'll be out in a minute."

"Okay."

Tim walked over to the baby's room to check on him. He was playing comfortably with his toys.

Having done taking a bath, Angelina came out of the shower with a towel wrapped around her.

"Hi honey. Welcome."

"Who is the woman that opened the door for me?"

"Honey, that's the nanny. Her name is Lissandra. I just hired her. She will be our nanny and housekeeper."

"How and where did you meet her?"

"My friend Kikwana introduced her to me. She gave a very good recommendation of her. I'll introduce her to you in a few minutes. She is a very lovely lady and is very good with kids."

"Really? Where is she from?"

"She just came to the country. She is not legally authorized to work in the United States yet, but has applied for an authorization and is waiting for an approval."

"But how do you know she's good with children?"

"She has worked for one family before. The kid was very rough, but she handled him gently and effectively."

"And how much will we be paying her every week?"

"Well, she has agreed to accept $1,500.00 per week. She will be living with us. Her duties not only include taking care of our child, but also helping me in the house with all our housekeeping needs."

"That sounds good."

Angelina was beginning to get agitated with all these questions from Tim.

"Why all this?"

"I just wanted to know. After all, I will be the one paying her."

"So you don't trust me?"

Tim didn't want to offend her. He had to think of a way to lighten things up.

"Not that I don't trust you, but if she is going to be taking care of our child, I would like to make sure that she is somebody honest and trustworthy."

Angelina got even more frustrated after hearing this. She felt as if Tim doubted her capability to raise a child by herself or was simply careless."

"Are you trying to say that I don't care about our child?"

"No."

"Then what do you mean? That I can't take a good decision?"

"Not at all honey. I trust your judgment. I respect your decisions."

"I'm glad you do, and I'm sure you know damn well that I'm not stupid. There's no way in the world that I would hire someone who can't take care of my child."

"But I never said that. I was just asking a normal question. A question anybody can ask. I'm mostly concerned about our baby."

"I'm concerned about him too. More concerned about him than you are. I'm the mother, for God's sake. I carried him in my womb for nine months. If anybody is concerned about him, I am the one."

"You are right Angie, but you have to understand that I'm his father too. I'm equally concerned about him just as you are and have the right to know the character of someone who will be taking care of him."

"I'm sure you do. But let's end this conversation right now. I don't want to hear it anymore," Angie said, pointing her fingers toward Tim's face.

Tim walked away quietly into the bedroom. As he began to undress, Angelina worked toward him.

"Honey, you know this is her first week on the job, and right now, she has no money on her. When I hired her, I told her that I will pay her this week's salary in advance. I would like to follow up on my promise."

"You have our debit card. You can withdraw up to two thousand dollars each day from the card. Use it and withdraw the $1500.00 for her weekly salary."

"Okay honey. I'll take care of that."

Lissandra was in her room, listening quietly to the conversation between Angelina and her husband. But she kept quiet. That was the right thing to do because she was not expected to get involved in a family matter, and she didn't even know Tim yet. They never officially met. Their first encounter was when she opened the door for him.

Angelina walked toward Lissandra. She was sitting in the living room. She sat beside her and called Tim.

"Honey!"

"Yes?" Tim answered.

"Come over here please."

"Okay."

Tim walked toward the women.

"Tim, this is Lissandra."

"Hi,", Tim softly responded.

"Hello," Lissandra replied and Angelina continued.

"Lissandra, this is my husband Tim. I'd like to introduce the two of you to each other. Honey, Lissandra will be our nanny. She'll be taking care of our baby and the house."

"Oh great. Welcome Lissandra. I'm sure you and my wife will get along pretty well. She said some very good things about you. Once again, welcome to the house."

"Thank you, sir."

Tim walked away and Angelina followed behind him, smiling as they walked to their bedroom. They laid down and dosed off during the night.

Fourteen

This morning, Tim got up, got dressed and left straight to work. Mrs. Branch was sitting in the living room, watching television, when suddenly, the house phone rang. She picked up the handset and answered.

"Hello?"

"Hello Angelina, this is your mother calling."

"Hi mom."

"Everything is fine. I just wanted to inform you that your dad has fully recovered. He's doing much better right now."

"Oh! Thank God."

"Thank God for the help you gave us."

"It's dad. I must help whenever I can."

"I'd like to thank your husband as well. How is he doing?"

"Yes. He's doing really fine. He's at work right now, but I will let him know that you called and wanted to thank him. I'll make sure he gets your message."

"Mom, how's brother Sunny doing?"

"Sunny is doing great. He is currently engaged to a woman he met at a night club. After he became involved with his fiancee, he told us that he found a job with a construction company."'

"A construction company?"

"Yes. A construction company he said."

"What kind of construction company?"

"According to him, a building construction company owned by Nigerians. They design and build new residential homes and remodel existing ones."

"Oh. That's great."

"Yes. We are all happy with his progress."

"Yes. Where is he now?"

"He has moved to the city. He now lives in Manila, from what we know."

"Do you still have any contact with him?"

"Yes. We have his phone number. He said we can reach him there anytime. But since he left, we haven't heard from him that much."

"Alright. May I have his number? I would like to talk to him if possible."

"Okay. Hang on a minute."

Felicia, Angelina's mother, went to the back of her house. She brought out her handbag and searched through it for her phone book. She couldn't find it. It wasn't there. She went back to the living room and located her phone book. It was on the table next to the chair. She picked it up, went through it a couple of times, and found Sunny's telephone number.

"Are you still there, Angie?"

"Yes mom."

"I found his number."

"Okay, let me have it."

She gave her the number over the phone. Angelina wrote the number down on a piece of paper she had in her hand.

"Okay mom. I got it. I will call him sometime later to check on him. I have some important things I would like to discuss with him.

"Okay Angie. Good luck to you. Don't forget us over here. You know how bad the situation was before you left. It has gotten even worse now."

"Don't worry mom. I'll keep in touch."

"Bye for now." They hung up.

Angelina felt good about the conversation. She was glad to hear that her father had recovered from a life-threatening illness and that her brother was engaged and had moved out of the house, permanently employed in the city of Manila. Everything seemed to be working out fine for the family she had left behind in the Philippines. She was eager to hear from her brother Sunny.

She took out her cell phone and immediately dialed her brother. The phone rang. Sunny looked at the number on the caller identification screen of the phone unit to see if he recognized the caller. It was an international call, from the United States, and he wasn't sure who it was. The identification only displayed the number; the name of the caller was not displayed. Sunny usually screened his calls before he accepted or rejected them. He accepted calls only from people he knew or was doing business with. He did not accept the call from Angelina, not knowing at the time who it was. The call went to his voice mail. Angelina did not leave a message for Sunny. Instead, she dialed the number once again, and Sunny once again did not accept the call. It went to the voice mail. This time, Angelina decided to leave a message on his voice mail.

"Sunny, this is your sister Angelina calling from the United States. You can reach me at this number. Hope to hear from you soon."

She hung up and continued in anger, "Shit. He's not picking up his calls. I'll wait and see if he calls back."

Just about ten minutes later, her phone rang. She looked at the caller identification number to see if she recognized the caller; however, the number did not display. It was a private caller, but she decided to accept the call anyway.

"Hello?" she spoke into the phone.

"Angelina, this is sunny. I got your message. You can call me back now."

He immediately hung up because he didn't have enough money to make a long-distance call. Angelina was excited to hear from him. She called him right back and he answered.

"Hello Angie. Sorry, I didn't know that was you the first time until I got your message. How are you doing?"

"I'm fine."

"It's good to hear from you again."

"Yes. Likewise. I'm so happy to hear from you as well."

"Since you went to America, we haven't really spoken."

"Yes. But I usually call home. And when I asked about you, mama told me you moved out of the house."

"Yes. I had to make a move out of there. You know how poorly we lived, poor, and mum does not work. We slept in one living room together. It got so bad that I decided to look for a job and found one."

"Yes. Mom also told me that you are now engaged. Is that true?"

"Yes. It is very true. Women always rejected me because I had nothing to offer them. One night, I went to a night club and met a very beautiful woman. I approached her gently and she accepted me. We began dating and fell in love with each other. We finally got engaged and are hoping to get married soon."

"Oh, that is a great thing. I am so happy to hear this. You are finally getting settled. Mum also told me that you are now employed."

"Yes. That is exactly true. I work as a builder for this construction company. The owner is a Nigerian. I started out as a laborer. But the owner admired my hard work and trained me, finally promoting me to a managerial position. We build, remodel and sell houses. We built and sold several houses. We are very good at what we do."

"This is good to know. I'm so proud of you Sunny. My husband is quite rich and we are living a good life here in America. I want to build a big and beautiful house in Manila. I hope to stay there whenever I visit the Philippines. Perhaps, I would like to retire there someday."

"Well, you are in the right hand. The place I live in with my fiancée is a mansion. It cost quite a lot but I was able to finish it without a lot of hassle. I spent more than seven hundred thousand to build this house. I can certainly help you in any way to achieve your dream to build a big house."

"Alright, good. I'd like my house to have a swimming pool, a gym, a tennis court and a garage."

"Okay. I got it. I know you have a good taste of luxury and I am here to make it happen. A house of that nature will cost approximately one and a half million dollars to complete. Is that something you think you can afford?

"Yes. That should not be a problem at all."

"Okay Angie. I'm happy to hear that. There is currently a land available in the plain fields of the city here. Most rich people here in Manila lives there. The former president's wife also resides there. This particular land is currently vacant and will be suitable for the kind of house you want to build. Do you still remember the former first lady of the Philippines?"

"Of course, yes. The flamboyant woman."

"Yes. That's where your proposed property is located. Based on my good knowledge of the land and experience in building and construction, the architect will charge about $100,000.00 just to draw the plan."

"Okay. Now how do I get the money over to you?"

"That's the easiest part. I will give you my bank account number, and whenever you are ready, you can wire the funds to that account. You don't have to send the entire funds at a time; you can send $25,000.00 first as a retainer for the architect. Once he completes the drawing, you can send the remaining balance."

"That sounds good to me. I will send the $25.000.00 to you as soon as possible."

"Okay. I'll be on the lookout for the money, and I will email you a copy of the proposed plan when finished."

"Thank you Sunny."

Angelina was happy with the conversation she had with Sunny. She began walking up and down in the living room. She clapped her hands together, grinning ear-to-ear. She sat down on her recliner chair where she usually watched television and began searching for her favorite shows. After a short while watching television, she felt a little thirsty and called the housekeeper. "Lissandra?"

"Yes Angie."

"Make me a cup of coffee and lightly toasted bread please."

"Okay Angie. It will be ready in a moment."

Lissandra went to the kitchen, prepared the toast and coffee, and brought them over to her. She sat relaxed and ate quietly. When finished, she felt a little dizzy and fell asleep on the couch.

Fifteen.

It was about 7.30 a.m. in the morning. Tim and Angelina had just woken up. Tim was beginning to get ready for work. Angelina was still lying on the bed. Tim went to the bathroom, took a quick shower, and came right out. He got dressed and was on his way out to work.

Angelina just got up from bed. She made breakfast and sat eating while watching television at the same time. She glared at the clock as it was approaching 12.30 p.m. She felt she had nothing else to do at home and would want to get out of the house for some time. She hadn't perfected driving yet. She still had minor issues with parallel parking. Keeping that in mind, she decided it was just the right time to go practicing. She picked up the phone and called the driving school. The receptionist picked up the call.

"Hello, how may I help you?" the receptionist enquired.

"Hello. I'm Angelina Branch, one of your students. I would like to have my instructor Brian pick me up today for a driving lesson."

"Sorry, Mrs. Branch. Brian Shay no longer works for our company."

"Why?"

"He's being fired, but we have several instructors, and I can dispatch one of them to come to you immediately. Would you want me to schedule you with another instructor?"

"Not right now. I will call you in a few minutes should I decide to continue."

"Thank you. Hoping to hear from you soon." They hung up.

Angelina stood silent for about three minutes after hanging up the phone. She walked toward her bedroom and picked up her hand bag. She took out her phone book from the hand bag and began looking for Brian's contact information. He had given her his phone number and address. She found his number and called him. When the phone rang, a woman answered and said.

"Hello?". Her voice was pale. Angie figured out that it must be a woman in her early or mid-seventies. She didn't immediately think it was Brian's girlfriend or wife who answered. She hesitated for a second and then said,

"Is there a Brian Shay there?"

"Yes. I'm his mother. Hold on a moment while I go get him," the woman responded. Angelina felt a little relieved as she didn't want to create any pandemonium for Mr. Shay

The Shays had a cordless phone device. Brian resided in the basement of the house, so his mother had to go down there to get him. She took the phone to Brian.

"Brian, you got a phone call."

"Thanks mom. Who's that anyway?"

"Sorry, I didn't ask."

She handed the phone over to him and walked back to her room.

"Hello," Brain said.

"Hello. Is this Brian Shay?"

"Yes. Who's this?"

"This is Angie, your former student driver."

"Hi Angie, I've been thinking about you."

"Thank you. I had called your office and was told that you are no longer there."

"Yes. I quit. Them guys ain't right. They don't pay very well. I got tired of their games, so I decided to quit."

Brian wasn't telling her the truth. He was fired because of cocaine possession. Another student driver noticed that Brian was high on drugs on the job and notified his company. His supervisor immediately inspected the vehicle and found traces of cocaine vials. He was effectively terminated.

"Well, I have improved much in my driving, but there are still a few areas that I would like to perfect. I still have problems with parking."

"Most people do. You are not alone. I'm available to help you whenever you are."

"You are?"

"Of course, yes. With a learner permit in your possession, I can still teach you. A lot of people don't use driving schools anymore, to be honest."

"When are you available?"

"Anytime you are ready. I can come now if you want. I got nothing else to do. I gotta tell you, I'm so glad you called."

"Do still remember where I live?"

"Yes, I remember."

"How long will it take you to get here?"

"About thirty minutes."

"Okay, come over. I'll be outside waiting for you."

"I'm on my way."

"See you in a bit."

Brian was so happy to hear from Angelina. He had waited patiently for her. He quickly got ready, then went up to his mother and gave her the phone.

"Thanks mom. That was one on my former student drivers."

"Yea?"

"Yea. She wants me to continue teaching her how to drive. It seems like a I got a new job."

"That's right, son. Don't act foolish again."

"No mum. I gotta get my shit straight this time."

"You better, or else you'll be doomed."

"That's right. Mum, can I get $20.00. I gotta hop on the train to go meet her. I'll pay you back this time."

"It's about time. You've been out of work for a while," she said, as she walked over to get $20.00.

Brian quickly ran out of the house and went straight to the subway station. There, he purchased a one-way ticket, walked over to the subway platform, and waited for his train. The train arrived in about five minutes. Brian got into the train and was well on his way to meet his student Angelina Branch.

Angelina was inside her house watching television. She looked at her wristwatch. It had been more than ten minutes since she first spoke to Brian. After a little while, she walked toward the door to check if anybody was waiting outside, but nobody was there, so she went back into the house. She looked at her watch again and saw that twenty-five minutes had passed since she last spoke to Brian. She figured out that he would have been there, so she walked downstairs toward her vehicle. She got inside the vehicle and sat there waiting.

She looked toward the rearview mirror and saw a man walking hastily toward the vehicle. It was Brian. She smiled softly. Brian walked toward the passenger side of the vehicle. Angelina clicked the door locks from inside to unlock the door while Brian pulled the door open and got inside the vehicle.

"Hi Brian," she said, as she immediately began driving away.

"Hi! How are you?"

"Great. I just thought I have to do this."

"I'm glad you thought about it and decided to do it. But hey, it's good to see you again," Brian said, as he leaned over to kiss her on the cheek. "Look at you. You're driving almost like a Pro."

Angelina laughed out very loud and said, "Yes. I've gotten better over time. I'm only having one problem – parallel parking."

"Parallel parking is one area most learners always have a problem with. Therefore, you are not alone. But don't even worry about it; we'll take care of it."

Sixteen

Angelina and Brian had driven about one block away from her residence when Brian came up with an idea. He thought about the best place suitable for the lesson.

"Why don't we go to the same old place where I taught you the last time?" Brian asked.

"Okay, that's fine," Angelina said, as she continued to drive toward that direction. It was about two miles away. It was a good road to learn driving, especially parallel parking.

"How is the family?"

"They are alright. My son is doing very good right now. He's growing pretty fast."

"Great. How about your husband?"

"He's fine I guess. He left us all home as usual and has gone off to work. We are not really getting along very well. I'm simply tired of his nonsense and wanna get out of this relationship."

"Hmm. Most men are just like that. They think women don't know any better."

"Last night we got into an argument over some nonsense and he pushed me. I fell toward the chair in the living room. I almost broke my skull."

"He did?"

"Yes. He did."

"Are you serious? He can get into some real problem with this kind of behavior. You know, if you had called the cops, they would have arrested him. You can press charges against him if you want to."

"I don't wanna go through that right now. What I really need is an apartment of my own, where I can go to sometimes when he's out for work."

"That shouldn't be a problem at all. My sister works for a real estate company. They help people find apartments very quickly. You can move in anytime you are ready."

"Do you have her number?"

"Sure. It's my sister. I can call her for you right now."

"Do that then."

She handed her phone over to Brian. He dialed his sister on the phone.

"Hello?"

"Hello Melissa, this is Brian."

"Hi Brian. You got a new number now?"

"No. I'm calling from my student's phone. I've got some questions for you."

"Go ahead."

"Do you have any apartments for rent?"

"Yes. I got a couple of them. You're looking for a place for yourself?"

"No. For my friend."

Melissa laughed briefly. She wondered if her brother was looking for a place to rent when he doesn't have any job.

"I thought it was for you. I was wondering if you have gotten another job."

"No. Not yet. but I'm still looking."

"Yes. I have some beautiful apartments available for rent to qualified individuals, one of which is a two-bedroom flat on the east coast. The building was just recently renovated. It has all kinds of amenities, including a gym, washing machines, and much more. The monthly rental is $950.00."

"Alright Melissa, hold a moment, I gotta speak to my friend. As a matter of fact, I'll call you back as soon as we are done talking."

"Alright. Thank you."

Brian hung up, but still had the phone on his hand as he was beginning to explain to Angelina what he heard from Melissa.

"She's got a two-bedroom apartment in the east coast, similar to where you live now. The east coast is a very beautiful place. Inside the apartment is a gym and washing machines and a lot of other things that makes it very comfortable to live in. There is a playground in the backyard designed especially for children, just like something you would love, and she's asking for just $950.00 per month."

"That sounds like a deal. I can rent the place from her almost immediately."

"Okay sweetie. I'll let you talk to her yourself, and the two of you can arrange when you can see the place."

Brian redialed Melissa's number, and at the first ring, handed the phone over to Angelina.

"Hello Brian."

"Hello. This is Angelina, Brian's friend."

"Oh sorry. Hi Angelina."

"Hi Melissa. Brian just told me about the apartment you have available on the east coast."

"Yes. It's a two-bedroom apartment. Newly renovated. It has all kinds of stuff you can think of. It is really a very nice place. If you are interested, you can move in immediately. You'll need to pay one month's rent and one month's security deposit plus a one-time brokerage fee of $950.00, bringing it to a total of $2850.00."

"What kind of payment do you accept?"

"We accept all forms of payments – cash, credit, or debit card and money order."

"That sounds good to me."

Angelina wanted to know about the methods of payment. She did not want to use check or credit card for the payment because her husband Tim would see the transaction and may discover her plans.

"When can I see the apartment?"

"You can see it at any time today, but I am now at another location with a potential renter, on an open house, but we will be finished in the next hour. After that, I'll be free for the rest of the day. I can arrange to meet you at the place this evening at around 7.00 p.m. if you want."

"Sure, no problem. 7.00 p.m. tonight is just fine for me."

"Okay. I'll text you the address and directions on how to get there as soon as we hang up. I hope to see you then at 7.00 p.m."

"Thanks. See you then."

They hung up and she was now waiting to receive the information. As she waited, she immediately turned over to Brian.

"Brian?"

"Yes sweetie?"

"That was quick and easy."

"Yes. My sister is very responsive. She knows her job well. She is good at what she does. She grew up like that. Everybody in my family is very successful. They work very hard."

"That's good to know."

Angelina was slowly learning how to parallel park. But Brian had something else in mind. He wasn't sure if she would permit him to go with her to her appointment with his sister Melissa. So, he decided to ask.

"Sweetie? Do you mind if I go with you?"

"Oh sure. You are the one who made the connection in the first place. I don't even know her by face, although now I know her by voice."

"Okay. Thanks. I'm just asking."

He paused for a while and looked at her straight in the eye with a gentle smile on his face and said, "I would really love to be your man."

She laughed and tapped him in the back and said.

"You know I'm still married."

"I know that fully well, but that doesn't matter to me anyway."

"Okay. We'll see how that goes."

Her phone blinked. She got a signal for a text message. She pulled over and stopped to read the message.

"She just texted."

"She did?"

"Yes. It's here."

It was the message she was waiting to receive from Melissa.

She looked at her wristwatch. It was about thirty minutes to the hour. She put the address on the GPS. She seemed to be in a hurry.

"Brian, we have got to start heading there right now. It's almost 7 o'clock."

"Okay, let's go."

They immediately drove toward the destination. Melissa, like most agents, was already there, awaiting their arrival. When they arrived, they got out of the vehicle and were received by Melissa.

"Hi Melissa."

"Hello Angelina. Good to see you. I'm glad you made it on time. Alright, let's walk up this way and you can take a look at the apartment."

They walked upstairs and into the apartment. Angelina looked at the apartment. She seemed to love it.

"This is a beautiful place. I know I'm going to take it. I'll meet up with you tomorrow in your office for the payment and the lease agreement."

"See you then," Melissa said, and all of them both drove off.

Seventeen.

It was late in the evening when Tim Branch returned home from work, but Angelina was not at home. At first, he didn't realize it.

"Angelina!" he yelled out, but got no answer. He went into her bedroom, looking to see if she was sleeping, but found the room empty. He walked back into his room and began to undress as he wondered where she was at that time of the day. After getting undressed and putting on his evening clothes, he walked to the living room. The house was just quiet.

"Lissandra!" Tim shouted out. "Are you there?"

"Yes Tim. I'm in the toilet. I'll be out there in a minute."

"Okay," Tim said.

He took out his cell phone and dialed Angelina's number. Her phone rang more than six times, but went answered. He hung up and sat on the living room chair. He whispered to himself.

"Where can she be? Perhaps to the grocery? Her phone battery may have died. But no, it did go to the voicemail."

Lissandra had just finished using the toilet and she walked upstairs toward the living room where Tim was sitting.

"Hello Mr. Branch. Welcome."

"Lissandra, did my wife tell you where she went when she was leaving?"

"Yes sir. She went for her driving lesson. That's what she said on her way out."

"I had called her twice on her cell phone but it went to her voice mail after it rang a couple of times. I'm concerned about her safety right now."

"May be she is in an area where the network is less or perhaps, she doesn't have her phone with her."

"Well, I hope nothing has happened to her. That's just my concern right now."

"Oh no, Tim. Don't worry so much. I hope she's alright. I'm sure she's safe."

Tim went back to his bedroom. In his bedroom, he had a small office table by the right end side. He usually used that little space for minor jobs that he wasn't able to finish at work. He sat down, opened his bag, and began counting the money he had made for the day, getting it ready to be deposited in the bank the next day. He had thirty thousand dollars in his bag. That was just the cash transaction for the day. By the time he had finished counting the money, the doorbell rang. Angelina had just arrived home from her driving lesson.

Lissandra ran to the door and opened the door for her and she walked into the house, walking toward the room where Tim was sitting. As soon as Tim saw her, he welcomed her home.

"Hello honey," Tim said, as Angelia approached.

"Hi honey. I just got back. It was a heck of a day. I went to practice driving. We left out late. There was a lot of traffic out there today going back and forth. The police got involved. They had to clear the traffic, thereby causing heavy back log, resulting in a standstill for hours."

"I called several times, but you didn't answer. Your phone rang each time I called, but when you didn't answer, it went to the voice mail."

"You called?"

She had intentionally switched off her phone. It was on an airplane mode. She pretended as if she didn't know where her phone is and started looking for it inside her bag and suddenly found it and took it out and began checking for a missed call.

"Sorry honey. I didn't realize the ringer was off."

"No problem, honey. I was just making sure that you are alright. I know you never usually stayed out this late."

"Thanks honey. You are such a sweet heart."

She went closer to him and kissed his cheek, and then walked over to her bedroom and began to undress. After she had finished undressing, she put on her evening clothes and walked back over to Tim.

"Honey, what do you want for dinner tonight?"

"Anything that pleases you is just fine for me. I'm not really that hungry tonight. Perhaps, a plate of rice and fish will be alright for me."

"Okay honey. I'll have it ready in a short time."

Tim decided that it was time to take a shower. He went into the bathroom for his evening bath. He turned on the faucet and the water began to flow. Angelina heard the water running and began to walk toward the bathroom where Tim was about to take a bath.

"Honey, are you in the shower?"

"Yes, honey. I need a long bath tonight, but I'll be out in a bit."

"Okay. Take your time."

Angelina walked out of the bathroom and went inside Tim's bedroom. She looked around and saw his briefcase beside the night stand, sitting by the small computer table beside the dresser. She opened it quickly and saw a stack of cash inside. She slowly closed the briefcase and put it back exactly at the same spot she picked it up from and quietly walked back to the kitchen area.

Tim had just finished bathing. He walked out of the bathroom and went straight to the dining room. The dinner was already on the table waiting for him. As soon as Tim sat down on the dining chair, Angelina walked over and sat beside him. Tim wasn't feeling so well. He felt weak and knew he was coming down with some kind of illness. He felt that it was the right thing to let his wife know about it.

"Honey, I'm not feeling so well tonight."

"Why? Is there something wrong?"

"I feel constantly dizzy and weak. I have pain all over my body."

"That sounds like some kind of illness. Why don't you go the hospital for a checkup?"

"I can wait till tomorrow, but if it continues, I'll go to the clinic."

"Honey, I think you should go to the hospital right away. I don't want you to wait till tomorrow. Tomorrow may be too late."

While Angelina was still talking, Tim lowered his head on the dining table. Angelina walked away quickly to her bedroom. She dressed up very fast, went over to Tim's room and picked up his shoes and a pair of jeans.

"Honey, get up. Get up, please. We've got to go to the hospital."

Tim slowly got up and put on his jeans and Angelina helped him put on his sneakers. She picked up her car keys and walked downstairs toward the car. She opened the passenger side of the car and Tim got into the vehicle very slowly. She ran over to the driver side, got inside the vehicle, turned on the ignition and sped away to the clinic. They got to the hospital within fifteen minutes. As soon as they arrived at the hospital, Angelina helped Tim out of the vehicle and led him to the emergency section, straight to the receptionist.

"Hello fellows, how may we help you today?" the receptionist said.

"I feel very weak and I have pain all over my body. I can barely function."

"Sorry to hear that. You can have a seat over here while I get someone to assist you."

Tim sat down while the receptionist paged the nurse. The nurse immediately came straight to him.

"Good evening sir."

"Good evening."

"I hear you are feeling weak and experiencing pain all over your body. I'm here to assist you. I'll need to take your blood pressure first."

The nurse brought out her thermometer reading, wrapped it around Tim's stretched arm. The reading began and came to a stop at a point. The nurse looked at it.

"Your blood pressure is very high and way above normal reading. Do you have a family history of hypertension?"

"Not that I know of."

"Okay, not a problem. I have to run a couple of tests before I can determine the course of your pain and weakness. Is that alright with you?"

"Yes. That's why I'm here."

She placed another reader on Tim's chest to check his heart rate. She felt it needed some attention.

"Okay sir. I think we have to keep you here until tomorrow to monitor your situation. The doctors have all gone home for the day."

"Okay."

"That's a good thing that he will be kept overnight," Angelina added.

Tim was admitted to the hospital this evening and Angelina sat there for a while with him. After two hours, she decided it was the right time to go home. She kissed him on the cheek.

"Honey, I gotta go home now, but I'll be here in time tomorrow to check on you."

"See you tomorrow."

"Goodnight honey; feel better."

Angelina walked away from the room to the parking area of the hospital, got into her vehicle and drove straight home. When she got home, she went straight to the bedroom and picked up Tim's briefcase. Inside the bag was a stack of cash. She opened the bag and removed all the money in it and began to count them. She counted them in stacks of thousands. It totaled $30,000.00. She put the money in her handbag, locked Tim's briefcase, and placed it back in the position from where she originally picked it up. She smiled gently. She was happy with what she had found. She went into her living room and hid her handbag inside the closet where nobody may see it and she went straight to bed for the night.

Eighteen.

This morning, Angelina woke up and took a bath. She decided it was time to speak to Melissa. She picked up the phone and dialed her number.

"Hello?"

"Good morning Melissa. It's Angelina Branch. Do you have a moment?"

"Yes, Mrs. Branch. Are you ready to take the apartment?"

"Yes Melissa. I'm ready."

"Okay, great. The first thing that needs to be done is for you to come down to my office and sign the lease agreement, and then pay the required down payment. Do you still remember how to get here?"

"No, but I can find out."

"Will you be driving or coming down by the subway?"

"I think I'll drive."

"Okay, great. I'll text you my address just as we speak and you can put in on your GPS."

"Okay. I'll wait for your text message."

Melissa went to her computer and sent her address to Angelina. Angelina held on to her cell phone as she waited for the text message to come through. In less than a minute, her cell phone received the text message signal and she was alerted.

"Hold on Melissa, it seems the message is here. Let me check my mail box."

"Okay," said Melissa.

Angelina put Melissa on hold for a little while she began to check messages.

"Yes, it came through," she said to herself as she switched over to Melissa.

"I got the address. I'm heading over there now."

"Alright, see you soon."

Angelina got into her vehicle and drove all the way to Melissa's office. It was about a half-hour drive. When she arrived at the building, she parked her car at the valet parking. She exited her vehicle and walked toward the building through the security check and walked into the elevator. Melissa's office was on the eighth floor of the building. She exited the elevator and went into Melissa's office. Melissa was there to meet and greet her.

"Hi Mrs. Branch, you got here faster than I expected."

"Yes. The traffic was smooth."

"Great. I can tell you didn't have any difficulty getting here."

"Not at all. My GPS is quite accurate. Thanks for this new technology."

"Welcome. You can have a seat here."

"Thank you."

Angelina sat down while Mellissa went to her cabinet, opened it, and brought out the lease agreement with the rider attached to it.

"Mrs. Branch, here is the lease agreement. It is a basic lease agreement, which describes all the information we discussed earlier. It is a two-year lease agreement that automatically renews every two years unless terminated by the landlord or the tenant in accordance with the stated terms and conditions. You can take some time and go through it."

"Okay."

She handed the lease to Angelia and she sat a little backward and relaxed as she began to read the lease, it's terms and conditions and the attached rider. She seemed to be comfortable with the agreement, and handed the form back over to Melissa.

"Okay. That looks good," responded Angelina.

"Do you have additional questions?"

"Not really."

"Okay. You can sign your name here by the dotted line."

She handed the form back to Angelina. She took the form from her and placed it on the table, signed it, and handed it over to Melissa.

"Thank you. Now it's time to make the deposit requirement. Are you ready to do that now?"

"Yes."

She reached inside her bag, took out the $2850.00 in cash, counted it and handed it over to Melissa. She took the money from her and counted it herself. It was complete. She wrote a receipt of the amount.

"Okay Mrs. Branch, here is your receipt and the key to the apartment.

"Thank you."

She took the receipt and the keys and left the office and began walking down to the parking lot. When she got to the parking lot, the parking attendant brought her out to the exit area. She reached into her handbag, took out a $5.00 bill, and handed it to the attendant as a tip.

"Thank you," the attendant said, as he accepted the tip.

"You're welcome."

She drove away. As she was driving home, her phone rang. She looked to see who's calling. It was Tim calling. She picked up her cell phone and answered.

"Hello honey, how are you doing?"

"I'm doing fine. The doctor showed up for work this morning. They ran additional tests and checked on me and said everything looked good, but they prescribed some painkillers for me that I should take every four hours, and I was discharged."

"That is good news. I was heading that way now before you called. I'm still on the way and hope to be there quickly, depending on the traffic."

"Okay. I'm at the waiting area of the hospital."

"Alright. I'll be there shortly."

As she continued to drive to the hospital, she thought about something. She thought that she had to hide the apartment lease and the keys. She whispered quietly to herself, pulled over to the side curb, removed the key and the lease agreement, and hid them in the trunk of the vehicle. She lifted up the trunk mat and hid them securely under the mat. She got back to steering and continued to drive to the hospital.

When she arrived at the hospital, she called Tim to let him know that she had arrived. Tim looked at his phone but did not answer, knowing that she was there. Having spotted her vehicle, he began walking toward her. She saw Tim as he approached and hung up the phone. Tim opened the door and quickly got into the vehicle and Angie immediately drove away.

She slid over closer to Tim and kissed him on the cheek as she began to talk.

"Hello honey, how did it go?"

"Like I told you earlier, the doctor came and ran some additional tests and checked on me, but found nothing worth worrying about. They gave me some medication to take home and a prescription that may be refilled as needed. I feel great this morning and would like to go to work as soon as we get home."

"I'm glad to hear that. I was very worried about you last night. You never complained about illness since we've been together, and I didn't sleep last night when you did."

"Uh honey. Thanks for your concern. I feel great now and am ready to go."

They drove straight home. Tim got out of the vehicle first when they arrived and went upstairs. He looked at the clock; it was already 1.00 p.m. He thought he could still make it to work at least for a half day. His workers would be happy to see him. They were very concerned about his health. He picked up his car key and his bag very quickly, walked downstairs into his vehicle, turned on the engine, and waited for the vehicle to warm up.

Nineteen

Tim Branch placed his bag on the passenger seat on the front and began driving to work. He felt a little hungry. He left the hospital without eating and didn't get enough time after he came home because he was in a hurry to get to work. He decided to stop by a roadside restaurant to purchase something to eat. The restaurant only sold burgers, so he decided he wanted a sandwich. At first, he thought about driving through the restaurant's drive-through. He looked at the drive-through, but saw that it was a long line, and he didn't have much time and patience to wait. He winded his window glass down and stuck his head outside and looked straight inside the restaurant but did not see many people. The line inside the restaurant was much shorter than the drive-through line. He decided to go inside the restaurant instead.

He pulled up into the parking lot. A lot of cars were parked there as well. He was very concerned about getting in and out of the restaurant quickly and getting right back on the road. It cost a quarter for 15 minutes of parking time. He parked the car and put in a quarter in the parking device to buy fifteen minutes parking time and ran inside the restaurant and stood in line waiting for his turn. He left his bag, still sitting on the seat of the front side passenger of the vehicle. It was a little sunny and mild, so he had the driver side of the door window down. It was now his time to place an order.

"May I please have a cheeseburger and large fries?"

"What kind of drink do you want with that?"

"A small milk shake."

The attendant placed the order. A few minutes later, his order was ready.

"Your food is ready sir. It's $13.45."

Tim reached inside his pocket and pulled out a $20.00 bill and gave it to the attendant. The attendant accepted the money from him, opened the cash register and counted $6.41 change before giving it to him. Tim took the change and put it all inside a tip box located on top of the counter. He checked his food to make sure the order was complete, and it was just as he had ordered. He walked out with his food toward the parking lot where he parked his vehicle, opened the door of the vehicle, got in and drove away straight to work.

When he got to work, he was warmly received by his secretary and other well-wishers. They knew of his illness and that he spent one night in the hospital, and were concerned about his well-being. Tim walked into his office and sat down in his chair. He breathed a big sigh of relief. He looked around his table and began arranging documents that were left on his desk. He read some of them and afterward shredded them. They were not important. He picked up the bank deposit book on the table as well as his bag. He was getting ready to fill out the deposit slip to go to the bank and deposit the money that was in his bag. He opened the bag, intending to remove the money, but found no money in it. He looked furious and a little confused. He thought he had made an error. He opened the zipper on the inside of the bag to see if he put the money in there, but found none. He blew a mild sigh and sat still, thinking if he had kept the money somewhere else, at home or in the office perhaps. He felt sure that the money was in the bag. He couldn't believe his eyes. That was the first time he had lost money, and he was sure about where it was kept. He picked up the bag once again and shook it up, but nothing came out of it. He was now sure that the money was missing, but not sure how.

He sat still and began to think how and where the money could be. He remembered that when he went to the fast food restaurant, he had left the window of his vehicle down in the parking lot. He was convinced that the money was probably stolen while he was in the restaurant to buy food. He felt he would let his secretary know about this.

"Monica?" Tim shouted out.

"Yes Tim?"

"I have just lost the money I had in my bag."

"How did that happen?"

"The last time I left the office, I went home. But that same night, I wasn't feeling so good and was taken to the hospital by my wife where I spent the night and was released the next morning. My wife picked me up from the hospital and we drove straight home. Immediately, I picked up my handbag for work and made a quick stop at the restaurant where I bought lunch and came directly to work. But when I was ready to fill out the deposit slip, I realized the money was not in the bag."

"Really?" Why don't you go back to the house and check again to see if you left them somewhere there."

"I am sure it's not there. I never remove anything from my bag whenever I go home, unless I am ready to go to the bank."

"Have you spoken to the people in the house? Ask around. Ask your wife and see if anyone found any money laying around somewhere in the house."

Tim immediately thought of something else. He felt he should go back to the restaurant where he had purchased some food. He got up and started walking out toward the exit door.

"I'll be right back. I've got to run back to that restaurant real quick."

"Good luck."

Tim walked away quickly toward the parking area, got into his vehicle, and drove away very quickly to the restaurant where he had bought the food. When he arrived at the restaurant, he parked his vehicle in front of the place and looked around to see if there were any security cameras attached to the walls. He walked toward the parking lot and saw two security cameras, one facing the parking lot and the other facing the back of the building. He was very happy about it.

He walked into the reception area where he initially placed the order for the food. He saw the same cashier who had attended to him. He immediately wanted to talk to him.

"Can I speak to your manager please?"

"Yes sir. Just a minute. I'll get him for you."

The cashier walked back to his manager's office and informed him that a customer would like to talk to him. The manager came out almost immediately to meet the customer.

"Hello, may I help you?" the manager asked.

"Yes. You may. I was here earlier. I had a bag full of money that I had left in my vehicle when I walked in here to make an order."

As Tim mentioned a bag full of money, the manager opened his eyes very wide, and Tim paused a while, but continued.

"When I left here after making the purchase and got to my office, I realized that the money in the bag was missing, although the bag was intact. I came back here and realized that you have security cameras and was happy when I saw that. I'm wondering if you can look back in your security monitor to see if anyone was standing by the car and stole the money when the vehicle was parked there."

"Do you have a receipt for the purchase you made here?"

"Yes."

Tim handed the receipt over to the manager. The manager accepted the receipt from Tim and looked at it. He saw that the receipt was from their store. He saw also the time when the receipt was issued.

"I will allow you to view the security monitor but not now, due to company policies and procedures. This sounds like a crime to me, and you will have to inform the authorities first. They will create a file for you and they can come back with you and then view the cameras."

"Okay sir. Thank you. I will do like you said. I will go to them now and file the report, and hopefully, we will be back here together."

Tim left the restaurant, got into his vehicle, and drove straight to the local police station nearby.

When he got to the police station, he went straight to the desk officer and was ready to file a report regarding the incident.

"How may I help you?" the attending officer asked.

"I may have been robbed at the Malgolia's restaurant when I parked my vehicle to purchase some food."

"How did this happen?"

"It happened when I parked my vehicle and ran into the restaurant to get some food. After I left the place and got to my office, I realized that the money I had in the bag was missing."

"Since you were not physically robbed, we will need to dispatch a unit to the scene. Do you know if there are any cameras there?"

"Yes. There are cameras there on the walls."

"Go back to the restaurant where the incident allegedly occurred and we'll dispatch a unit there in a short while."

"Okay sir."

Tim left the station and drove back to the restaurant, waiting for the cops to arrive. Within thirty minutes, a police vehicle pulled up at the Malgolia's restaurant. They came out of their vehicle, viewed the area, and walked into the restaurant to see the manager. The manager saw the cops coming and knew almost immediately that Tim had complied; they waited for the police at the reception as they walked in with Mr. Branch.

"Gentlemen, we have to investigate a complaint that allegedly took place in this restaurant a short while ago and we will need your cooperation to view your security camera footage."

"Not a problem, sir."

The manager took them to the back of his office where the camera footage could be viewed. The cops and Tim reviewed the camera between the hours Tim first arrived at the restaurant and the time he left for his office. They saw when Mr. Branch arrived at the restaurant as well as when he left his vehicle parked and walked in and out of the restaurant. Nobody went inside or near his vehicle when it was parked.

"Mr. Branch, there is no sign of visible entry into your vehicle. This incident did not take place at this location, as you can see yourself in the footage. Sorry, we will not be able to help you."

"Thank you."

The cops went back into their vehicle and drove away. Tim stood by his vehicle a little while, wondering how this could have happened. He would never believe that his wife had stolen the money even if anyone had told him so. He could not even have thought about it.

He looked at his watch. It was getting late for the day. This was usually the time he left office for home. He'd gotten tired and confused and decided to go home for the day, feeling disappointed and disturbed.

Twenty.

Tim went home tired from going back and forth to the restaurant and waiting for the police to find out how the money had gone missing from his bag. When he arrived home, he opened the door and went inside. Angelina was in the living room watching television. Tim dropped his bag on the floor and sat down on the couch opposite his wife. He usually sat beside her whenever he returned home from work, but this time he didn't.

He looked subdued. Angelina winked her eye and looking toward him.

"Welcome honey. You don't look so good. What's the matter?

"I had $30,000.00 in my bag last night before I went to the hospital. After you and I came back from the hospital, I picked up the handbag and went straight to work. But when I got to work and was ready to fill out the deposit slip, I opened the bag to put the slip inside together with the money, but found out, to my greatest dismay, that the money is missing."

"Really?"

She was relaxed and unperturbed about the whole incident. She picked up the glass of red wine she was drinking and took a little sip. The cup of wine was half-filled.

"Yes," Tim replied.

"How did that happen?"

"I have no idea whatsoever."

"Did you go back to the restaurant where you purchased the said meal to check if by accident you left the bag open and it fell off the ground or somewhere else?"

"Yes, I did. I went back there. I got the police involved. I had to get the cops involved because the manager wouldn't allow me to view the security camera footage, because it is a violation of their company rules and procedures. The police came and we viewed the footage together, but no one had even gone near it."

"This sounds like a mystery to me. Are you sure you kept the money in the bag? Maybe you thought you did, but perhaps you never actually did. This whole thing sounds so silly to me."

"I am very sure the money was in the bag. This is my usual way of doing things, and something like this has never happened to me before. This is the first time I've experienced something like this."

Angelina picked up the glass of wine and took another sip.

"Well, there's always a first time for everything, and like you said, this is your first: perhaps, you can learn from this."

Tim sat back quietly but Angelina continued.

"Let me see that bag anyway."

Tim handed the bag to her. She stood up and looked at it with a somewhat stubborn look in her face.

"This bag doesn't even have a lock. It's just a briefcase. Tim, how can you be so stupid to leave money in a bag like this without a common lock? This is crazy. Did you even ask your workers, especially Monica, that secretary of yours? Perhaps they may have an idea where the money is or who stole it. This looks like an inside job to me."

"My secretary and I have worked together since I first started my business more than ten years ago. I trust her with all my heart. She's a devoted Christian and she is not capable of doing something like this."

"Well, you never know."

"When I spoke to Monica regarding this matter, she's the one that suggested that I come home and look around the house; perhaps, I may have dropped the money somewhere or somehow around the house, but

I didn't think so. Nevertheless, nothing stops me from looking around."

Angelina got very upset and got up from the chair. She stood closer to Tim, facing him.

"Is she suggesting that I stole the money? Oh, wait a minute. So now you and your secretary are beginning to frame me a thief?"

"No one said that, honey. It was only a suggestion that I had already thought of; I wanted to look around the house, although that I was certain that it could not have occurred here. That's why I went to the restaurant at first with the cops to review the video."

Angelina could not resist being angry. She raged increasingly, this time shouting out louder.

"You are a bastard. When I married you, I married you out of love and had a beautiful child for you; now you are calling me a thief?" she said, pointing at his face and crying.

She got even more violent and threw the glass of wine over his face. She then threw the glass at him, but he dodged it and the glass shattered against the wall. Tim started walking away from her as she became more violent. She picked up a ladle and continued to walk toward him. Tim turned around and saw her with the long spoon and got very nervous at this point.

"Stop Angelina. Stop it. Put the ladle down. What's the matter with you honey?" Tim asked, walking away from her.

"Oh, so you don't know what the matter is?"

"No!" Tim replied, as he continued trying to elude her.

"You know what the matter is. You are a coward. You know what the matter is."

"I don't understand you. I don't understand what you are doing. I really don't know what the matter is."

"Yes, you do. You bastard. You accused me of stealing your money."

"I never accused you of anything Angelina. I was only explaining to you what happened to me and the steps I have taken so far to look for the money."

Before Tim could finish the sentence, Angelina threw the ladle at him and it hit his right arm in his attempt to dodge it. She followed suit after him. Tim ran into the bedroom. He attempted to shut the bedroom door on her, but Angelina ran faster toward him and forced her way into the room. As Tim backed away from her, he fell backward into the bed and Angelina jumped on top of him and started hitting him with her fists.

"Stop honey. Stop!" Tim shouted over and over, but Angelina would not stop hitting him. Tim was raised by his father. He had advised him to never beat a woman. He understood the consequences of beating a woman, especially his wife. As a result, he was more restrained and concerned about defending himself from his wife's violent rage.

He held her left hand while he laid backward on the bed. She struggled to free her hand, but couldn't, and she spit over his face and attempted to use her right hand to strike him again. Tim was able to stop her by holding her right hand as well. He got up quickly, pushed her away, and ran off to the living room.

Angelina got up and ran after him, shouting, "You pushed me!"

She got a little tired from the struggling, went back into her bedroom, closed the door and lay down on her bed, crying. Her tears had wet the pillow.

Tim stood outside his door, begging her to open the door.

"Honey, stop crying. Open the door. Angie! Angie, please open the door for me. What's the matter?"

She kept quiet and would not open the door for him. Tim got tired and weary and sat down on the couch in the living room, trying to recover his breath.

After a short while, Angelina got up and opened the door. When Tim heard the crack of the door opening, he stood up thinking that she might attack him again. But this time, she walked right out of the room and walked into the bathroom. She turned on the faucet, picked up her wash towel, soaked it in warm water, and started wiping her fake tears.

Tim walked closer to the bathroom door and stood watching her wash her face. He was skeptical at first, but moved closer to her and placed his hands on her upper elbow and began to comfort her.

"Honey, are you alright? Why are you crying honey?"

She said nothing. Instead, she lifted her head, looked at him, and leaned on his shoulder, without a word.

"Honey, if I said anything that may have offended you, please forgive me. I didn't mean to offend you. I do not ever intend to offend you."

She walked back toward the bedroom and laid down on the bed. Tim sat behind her. She pulled him closer to her and started kissing him. She began to get horny as was Tim; he began to get erect. His penis began to stick out of his underwear. He attempted to pull his pants off, but Angelina pulled him closer to her with his pants half down. Tim couldn't wait to make love to his wife. She grabbed his penis and put it into her vagina and Tim started pushing it in and out. She moaned softly.

"Fuck me. Fuck me honey."

Tim was quite tired from the struggle and couldn't last very long. He ejaculated quickly and fell asleep for the night.

Twenty-one.

This morning, Tim woke up and took a quick shower. He slowly got dressed and was ready to go to work. He sat down in the living room and waited to catch the morning news before he left. He switched on the television and listened to the news. Angelina was still in bed, lying down, but not asleep. He watched the news for about ten minutes and got ready to leave. He got up and walked back into the bedroom where Angelina was lying down; he bent over and kissed her on the cheek.

"I gotta go now. I'll see you later in the evening."

"Bye," she said softly and turned her back over to the other side. Tim left the room and walked outside to the front of the house, got into his vehicle, and drove off to work.

Twenty minutes after Tim left for work, Angelina got up from the bed and immediately parked all her belongings and some other items from the house, loaded them inside her vehicle, and drove away from the house with her son Tim Jr. She moved into the new apartment she had rented from Melissa. She went to the local police precinct and filed a complaint against her husband for domestic abuse.

It was late in the evening and Tim finished working. At about the same time, he usually called Angelina before he left work. He called her to let her know that he was about to come home from work. Her phone rang, but she did not pick up. It went straight to her voicemail. He decided he would leave a message on her voice mail.

"Hi honey, I hope you're fine. I'm about to leave work right now. I'll see you when I get there. Love you."

He hung up and walked out of the office, straight to his vehicle. He got inside and turned on the engine. While waiting for the engine to warm up, he decided to call Angelina again. He thought she would have called him when she received his message. Her phone rang, but it went straight to the voicemail, a signal indicating that the phone was turned off. He hung up without leaving her a message. He smiled gently, because he felt that his wife didn't want to answer him because of the quarrel they had last night, and he drove away.

When Tim returned home, he noticed that her vehicle was not there. They usually parked their vehicles in front of their house. He knew right then that she was not at home. He walked upstairs into as well as around the house, but Angelina wasn't there. The entire house was empty. He noticed that Angelina had packed all her personal belongings from the house and left the premise.

"She has disappeared. She ran away," he said, walking all around the house.

He sat down on the couch in the living room. The house was so quiet. He could only hear the noise from cars passing by occasionally. He was still in a confused state of the mind. He picked up his phone, but it dropped out from his hand. He let it sit there for a while and then reached for his phone book. He took out his phone book from his bag and found Kikwana's phone number. He picked up the phone from the floor and dialed Kikwana. Her phone rang and she answered, "Hello!"

"Hello, this is Tim Branch, Angelina's husband."

"Yes. Mr. Branch, how are you doing?"

"Fine. Have you seen my wife Angelina?"

"No. Mr. Branch, Angie and I have not spoken in a long time. Why did you ask, if I may ask?"

"I called her several times but she hasn't answered. This is just unusual for her."

"Maybe she went out somewhere or her phone is dead. She may answer you later, perhaps. But sorry, I haven't spoken to her today."

"Okay, thanks." He hung up.

Tim felt so uneasy and confused that he decided to calm down a little bit. He felt that it was a good time to take a little nap. He attempted to take a nap, but couldn't. He got up and sat down with his head over his knees.

He thought about something and whispered to himself, "I'd better get the cops involved here."

He dialed 911 from his cell phone. The police department picked up immediately.

"Emergency, how can I assist you?"

"My name is Tim Branch. I just came home from work to realize that my wife Angelina Branch is not there. The house is entirely empty. All her personal belongings and some of my personal belongings are also missing."

"Okay sir, is there any sign of forceful entry to the house?"

"No. I feel my wife has run away from the house with our son."

"Did you try to contact her?"

"Yes, I did. Her phone rang, but she did not answer. I left her a message and she hasn't called back."

"Sir, hold on while I check our records."

The operator ran a quick check of the police record. She found that Angelina had visited the local police precinct. She filed a police report complaining of assault by her husband and had to leave the house in fear of her life.

"Mr. Branch, your wife Angelina went to the local police precinct earlier this afternoon. She filed a police report against you, stating that you pushed her during an argument between the two of you. She also claimed that you accused her of stealing $30,000.00 from you. She said in her complaint that she is now afraid of you and decided to stay away from you for some time."

"Thank you sir."

Tim hung up. He was in a state of disbelief. He couldn't believe what he heard. He dropped his cell phone on the table, went into his bedroom, and laid down on the bed, thinking all kinds of things.

Suddenly, his phone rang. He got up from the bed. He thought it was Angelina. He looked around for the phone and found it on the table where he had kept it initially. He picked up the phone and pressed the accept button.

"Hello?" he yelled out.

"Hello Tim," the caller said. It's his mother calling. He thought the call was from Angelina. He felt a little weary and was disappointed.

"Hi mom."

"Hi. I just called to check up on you. How is the family?"

"Mum, you can't believe what happened."

"What?"

"My wife ran away with our son."

"When did this happen?"

"Today."

"Why?"

"We had an argument yesterday. Later, I thought everything was alright. This morning I left for work. When I returned home in the evening, I noticed that some of my personal belongings and all of her personal belongings are missing. She is not home."

"Do you know where she may have gone to?"

"No mom. I have no idea whatsoever. But I contacted the police, and they told me that she left the house because she is afraid of me. She claimed that I pushed her during the argument."

"Did you push her?"

"Hell no! The only thing I did was that I tried to get away from her when she was attacking me. She almost struck me with a ladle."

"Has she gotten her permanent resident card? The green card? I remember that you told me that you had applied for it."

"Yes, she has."

Tim's mom had a similar experience in the past. Her husband was a foreigner. He had divorced her after he became a citizen. His mother believed that Angelina's ugly and violent behavior was a result of her having gotten everything she wanted from him.

"Most foreigners are like that. Once they get their green card, they run away. That's why most Americans don't marry them anymore. I told you about that woman before. That's why I didn't attend your wedding, because I knew it would end this way."

"Mum, are you suggesting that she married me just to become a citizen and not out of love?"

"Well son, you can answer for yourself."

"You know what? You may be right. All these problems started right after she got her green card."

He paused for a moment and continued, "Mom, I'm sorry that I felt angry toward you for not attending my wedding. I can now agree with you. I'll get back to you soon."

"Take it easy son, and be careful. Stay out of trouble."

"I will. Thanks mom."

Twenty-two.

Several weeks had passed by and Tim had not heard from Angelina. He hadn't received any phone call from her and had not spoken to his son. He had no idea of their whereabouts. He had lost a few pounds, thinking of her and his son. He loved them dearly and was very concerned about their safety.

He picked up the phone and called the Immigration and Naturalization Service. Mr. Gary Saturday was a close of friend of his. They had dealt with each other in the past and knew one another very well. Mr. Saturday picked up and answered the call.

"Hello, Mr. Branch. What can I do for you?"

Tim began to explain exactly what happened between him and his wife to Mr. Saturday.

"It's about my wife Angelina, the woman from the Philippines."

"Yea. I know your wife, that very beautiful woman. I was there when you wedded her. Have you forgotten?"

"No I haven't forgotten. Well, after she got her green card, she ran away with my son, and she stole $30,000.00 cash from my bag. I wish to get her deported."

Gary heaved a little sigh and said, "Tim, this is just a waste of good time, and I am sure you probably know that. Most foreigners, whenever they get their legal status right, end up leaving their spouse. There's not much you can do about that. And about the $30,000.00 cash that you said she stole from you, I'm sure you know damn well that she is your legal wife, right?"

"Yes."

"Then, this is a civil matter, not a criminal one. You have to take it up in the family court. Your best bet here is to file for divorce on the grounds of abandonment, and some of that money could be taken out of her share. Is that something you want to consider right now?"

Tim was shocked. He hated the idea of a divorce. He truly loved his wife, and for some time, he had also been in love with her. He just felt this way toward her now out of anger.

"So, you mean she cannot be deported?"

"Yes. She cannot be deported for that. You married her for love. Your relationship with her is a bona fide one. When you petitioned for her to obtain her legal status, you were given a list of documents to submit in order to establish a bona fide relationship. Such documents included joint ownership of assets, such as bank accounts, life insurance policies and property ownerships, etc., which both of you held in your names. Her status is irrevocable, based on your claims."

Tim scratched his head.

"Thanks Gary," Tim said and hung up.

The doorbell rang. Tim got up from the chair. He wondered who that may be. He thought Angelina was back. He went toward the door, hopeful. It was not Angelina. It was the mailman. He opened the door and the mailman extended his hand and gave him his mail and a green receipt, requiring a signature as proof of delivery. Tim accepted the mail and the receipt from the mail man.

"I just need your signature here," the man requested. Tim signed on the receipt and gave it back to him.

"Thank you."

The carrier left and Tim shut the door and walked back inside. He looked at the envelope. The sender's name and address were on the back of the envelope. It came from the family court. He was astonished, but began to open the letter as he walked back to the living room. He sat down and started reading the letter. It was a summons and complaint notice.

ANGELINA BRANCH (PLAINTIFF)

VS

TIMOTHY BRANCH (DEFENDANT)

ORDER OF PROTECTON

To the above named Defendant:

You are hereby notified to appear at the family court at the address below to answer a complaint filed by the Plaintiff seeking an order of protection against you. Failure to appear at the time and date scheduled below will result in a default judgment being entered against you. A warrant for your arrest may also be filed by the court.

He was shocked and in disbelief. This was his first time to receive a court summons for domestic violence. He read the letter over and over again and took note of its content. He dropped the mail on the cocktail table and sat back on the easy chair. After a little while, he dosed off. After a short while, he was woken by the faint noise of a car passing by. He thought to himself for a little while. He had never been to court and possessed no court experience.

Twenty-three.

Angelina had successfully moved into her new apartment with her son. With $30,000.00 in her pocket, she was in a quite comfortable state. It would last her for a while, for a few months. She was very happy with her new apartment and her new-found freedom but she was lonely and horny at times. There was no man by her side, at least for now.

She picked up the phone and dialed Brian, her driving instructor.

"Hello,", Brian answered.

"How are you doing?"

"Fine, I guess. Just sitting here doing nothing but watching television."

"It's got to be boring. Isn't it?"

"Yes"

"Why don't you come over? Perhaps we can go for some lessons."

"I'm on the way. Will be there shortly."

Brian got up, ran into the bathroom, and took a quick shower. He got out of the shower and got dressed very quickly and took off to meet Angelina. He got the invitation he had been waiting for.

In about an hour or so, he arrived at Angelina's new residence. He rang the bell and she buzzed him inside the building. He took the elevator up to her apartment and rang the apartment bell. She opened the door to meet him.

"Hey baby," Brian said, as he walked in to her apartment. They hugged each other.

"Hey. Welcome. You got here pretty fast huh!"

"Yes. You got it all furnished up already. It looks pretty good."

"You know I'm a woman. I love a nice-looking place. You can have a seat anywhere you like."

Brian sat down on the couch while she walked over to the other side by the kitchen area. She was wearing a black lingerie so visible you didn't have to look deep to see all her body parts. Brian watched lustfully. He couldn't control himself. He got up gently and walked closer to her. She turned and looked at him straight in the eye and felt a sense of connection there. He held her by the waist and pulled down to the couch. She hadn't had sex in a long time and she was dying for it. She felt like a total different person.

She laid down with her back on the couch, letting Brian do all the work as he got in between her legs. He lasted for a good while before he ejaculated. He cleaned himself with some tissues and dozed off, while Angelina went to the bathroom and cleaned out.

She felt relieved. She sort of liked Brian and had fallen in love with him. They had been in constant contact with each other for a while.

When Brian woke up, Angelina was sitting beside him and watching television.

"Honey, you just woke up?"

"You are sweet. You put me to sleep."

She laughed out loud and Brian continued.

"You are the best thing that ever happened to me."

"Thank you."

"How is it going between you and your husband?"

"Hmm. I left that bastard. I'm never going back to him again. He thinks I'm a fool. He's trying to scare me."

"Look, if he ever bothers you again, let me know, and I'll take care of him. I am your man now."

"You will? How?"

"Whatever you want, I can do to him. I can kill him if you want or rough him up any time."

"That's good to know. I'll keep that in mind."

"I'm tired of people treating women like nothing."

"Well, we have a court date coming up pretty soon. I have filed for an order of protection from him after he pushed me violently. I'll probably need a witness in court to prove my case."

"I'll be the witness."

"Do you think you can be a credible witness since you don't live in there?"

"Hell yea. I was your driving instructor at one time. Each time I came there, I have always picked you up from the house. I can say that when I came to your house to pick you up that day for your lesson, I heard you screaming out loud, 'Get away from me. Don't touch me. Stop beating me Tim.' I can also say that when I came to the house and rang the bell to get you for your lesson, you came out of the house crying and I saw blood all over your body."

"That sounds pretty good to me. I see why you and I are connected."

"You are right, honey. We have a lot in common."

Brian reached out to her and kissed her. She rested her head on his lap, while he slowly squeezed her thick breasts. She grabbed his hands and held them still. She was still sore from the previous activity and was not ready to engage in another session so quick. She got up very quickly and said.

"I gotta make a quick phone call."

"Right on baby."

She picked up her phone and called Kikwana. The phone rang and Kikwana picked up.

"Hello," Kikwana answered.

"Hello Kikwana, how are you doing?"

"I just woke up. I'm getting ready to do dishes."

"Guess what? I got a credible witness for the court case coming up between my husband and I."

"Who's that?"

"My driving instructor. You remember when I was learning how to drive?"

"Yes, I remember"

"One of the days, he heard me screaming while I was coming out of the house to get in the school vehicle. He's willing to testify on my behalf."

"That's a good thing. He must surely like you, huh?"

"I guess. But I can use him for this important purpose. You know how men are. They will do just about anything to get in that dress."

They laughed out very loud.

"You are surely right, especially yours."

She had found the perfect person for her games. She loved tricking men.

"It's almost a guarantee that the court will grant you order of protection which you are seeking for and well deserving of."

"Thank you."

"Remember to include child support in your petition."

"Of course. What is the child for then, if not for the support. That was the first thing I filed for, but in a separate petition, both to be heard by the same judge on the same day."

"You are all set then. Keep me updated."

"Thank you. I sure will."

They hung up. Angie walked back to the living room where Brian was sitting. It was late in the evening and Brain had no plans of going back home. He felt much better staying with Angelina. He went to the bathroom and took out the scrub brush. He began to clean the bathroom, the tubs and the sink. Angie walked toward the bathroom and stood in front of the door watching him clean.

"You are doing a great job. When do you intend to go home?"

"Honey, I have no plans for that now. I hope to spend the night with you."

"You can if you wish."

"You know I surely wish so. I wish this place will be for the both of us."

He continued with his work.

Twenty Four.

Tim woke up this morning. He looked at his watch. It was about 6.30 a.m. The court time was set for 10.00 a.m. He got up and went straight to the bathroom. He took a quick shower and began to dress up. He put on light blue suit and tied his tie. He went to the kitchen and boiled some water enough to make one cup of coffee. He drank the coffee with half a pound of cake. He looked at his watch again. He seemed to be working on schedule.

He usually got to his office at 9.00 a.m. in the morning, and the court house was about 30 minutes away from his office. He called his office and Monica received the call.

"Hello Mr. Branch."

"Good morning Monica. I'm heading down to the family court this morning. As a result, I'll be late to work today. I am not sure when it will be over, but I'll keep you posted."

"Okay sir. I'll take care of things. Good luck."

"Thank you. Don't forget to send in the bid for the project."

"No, I won't forget. As a matter of fact, I'm working on it as we speak. I'll get it in by mid-noon today."

"Thank you."

They hung up. Monica started to work on the bid as she promised. She looked it over and everything seemed to be like they wanted it. The deadline to submit the bid for the job his office seeked was today by 5.00 p.m. She double-checked the bid.

"It all looks good to me," she said, and faxed it over. The fax was successfully transmitted. It generated a receipt of acknowledgement of the transmission. She attached the receipt to the bid as proof of successful transmission.

Tim arrived at the family court. He arrived on time but without an attorney. As he looked for a place to sit down and wait until they were called, he saw Angelina sitting in the second row in the middle of the waiting area. He decided not to talk to her and found a space in the back row and sat down quietly. Angelina came with Brian and he was sitting next to her. Tim had never met Brian before and did not know that he was with Angelina. The court was full of people sitting and waiting for their time to see the judge.

Tim looked at Angelina, but she paid him no attention. Brian was not looking at him, but he knew that was him. He knew him by the pictures Angelina had shown him.

The judge was ready to begin. The court clerk went over to the waiting area and called out the case for Angelina and Tim Branch. Angelina got up and walked into the court room, Tim right behind her. They were seated.

"Mr. Timothy Branch," Judge Right said, and Tim stood up.

"Please raise your right hand."

Tim raised his right hand, and the Judge continued.

"Do you swear to tell the truth, the whole truth, and nothing but the truth?"

"Yes, I do."

"You may be seated."

Tim sat down.

"Mrs. Branch, please raise your right hand."

Angelina stood up and raised her right hand.

"Do you swear to tell the truth, the whole truth, and nothing but the truth?"

"Yes, I do."

"You may be seated."

Angelina sat down quietly, looking sympathetic, and the judge continued.

"Mr. Branch, your wife Angelina is seeking an order of protection against you. In addition, she is asking for full custody of your child Tim Branch Jr. Tell me what happened here."

Tim looked up at the ceiling and said, "Well, your honor, I really don't have much to say here, except that my wife has been acting very strange lately. I've never, at any time, beat my wife, and neither will I ever do so. This whole problem started when I came home after a short hospital stay and found $30,000.00 missing from my bag. When I told my wife about it, she got furious and started a quarrel with me.

I got really tired of that and walked away from her. When I left and came back from work the next day, I found out that she had left our marital residence."

"Thanks Mr. Branch. Mrs. Branch, do have anything to say about this matter?"

"Yes your honor, and I'm going to make it really short and simple."

"Thank you, Mrs. Branch."

"Your honor, I've had enough from my husband, who I loved very much. He usually beats me whenever we get into any kind of argument. And yes, you heard him right. He came back from work and claimed that he had $30,000.00 in his bag and that the cash was missing. He accused me of stealing the money. He threatened to kill me unless I admitted that I stole the money, apologized to him and gave him back the money."

"He said he would kill you?" Judge Right asked.

"Yes, your honor. He said he would kill me. He smacked me in the face and kicked me down the stairs. I am now afraid of my husband."

"Mr. Branch, do you want to kill your wife?"

"No."

"Did you say you would kill your wife?"

"No."

"Well, Mr. Branch, even though you claim that you do not want to kill her or say you would kill her, she said that you did, and she is afraid of her life. It's your word against her, and I have to be very careful here because your lives may be in danger. Both you and her. My job as a judge is to make sure that the interest of both the parties is protected. What is your occupation, Mr. Branch?"

"I am an entrepreneur."

"May I see your most recent income tax return?"

"Yes, your honor."

Tim handed his most recent tax return to the Judge. The latter looked at it thoroughly and did some calculations using a calculator. He then proceeded with questioning Angelina.

"Mrs. Branch, what is your occupation?"

"I'm currently unemployed, your honor."

"I'll be back shortly with my decision."

After about five minutes, the Judge was ready with her decision.

"It is hereby determined by this court that an order of protection is granted to the Plaintiff. Mr. Branch, you should stay away from her and your child, Tim Branch Jr. You should neither make any contact with her nor should you go near her place of residence. This order shall be in effect immediately and shall remain so for a period of one year.

"Mr. Branch, I have taken a good look at your personal income as reported in your tax return. After deducting the expenses, I have determined that you should pay to your wife, as support, the sum of $15,900.00 each month, beginning this month. This payment shall be made directly to the child support collection unit.

Now just as a reminder to you, the failure to abide by this order can result in a warrant being issued for your arrest. This is my final judgment. The court is now adjourned."

Angelina waited until Tim walked out of the court before she left. He looked furious, but it was not a surprise, because he understood clearly well how the family court system works. He seemed rather disappointed.

Angelina walked out of the court room. Brian was there waiting for her. She kissed him and they walked out of the court house happy, laughing and holding hands.

Twenty five

The judgment was rendered and the decision was final. Angelina returned to her apartment with Brian. She got what she wanted for now. She's got an order of protection against her husband, and more importantly, she would be receiving $15,900.00 each month in child support, which was enough for her to live the way she wanted to. She felt relaxed and very comfortable.

While she sat in her bedroom watching television, her phone suddenly rang. She looked at her caller identification first before answering it. It was Sunny, her brother from the Philippines. She smiled and answered.

"Hello."

"Hello Angie, this is Sunny."

"Hi Sunny."

"Hi, sister. Everything is well. I have just emailed you a copy of the building plan. It's ready for your review. Did you get it?"

"Okay. Hold on a second while I log on to the computer."

She walked over toward the computer, turned it on and entered her password so as to access her email. She opened it, reviewed the building plan, and was satisfied with it.

"Great! This is really good, a complete mansion," she said to herself. She resumed her conversation on the phone with Sunny.

"Sunny!"

"Yea."

"I received it. I looked at it. It's terrific. That's exactly what I want."

"I know what you want. I'm your brother."

"Yes, you do. I see that now."

"Alright, I'll need the money now and we can start building."

"Okay. I have your account number and the bank information. I will remit the money immediately."

"Okay. I will call you as soon as I receive the money."

"Okay."

As soon they finished talking, Angie logged on to the joint bank account she held with her husband and wired $1.5million dollars to Sunny's bank account in the Philippines for use in building a house for her over there. The transaction was successfully transmitted. The money was now in Sunny's bank account.

A couple of hours later, her phone rang and she answered. It was her brother calling to confirm that he had received the money.

"Hello?"

"Angie? I received the money. Thank you. I'll begin the construction of the house. With all the money we need now available, your house should be ready within six months. I'll keep you updated with its progress."

"Thank you."

Twenty six

Tim Branch had just arrived in his office. He was getting ready to start his normal everyday business. He turned on his computer and logged on to his email. He received a message confirming a successful transmission of 1.5 million dollars to a bank in the Philippines. He was shocked and couldn't believe his eyes. He read the email once again and the message was the same. He thought this could have been a bank error, but his account had been debited by 1.5 million dollars. He saw another scheduled transfer of $450,000.00, which was still in progress. He almost went crazy.

He knew only he and Angelina had access to the account. He picked up the phone and called his bank. Mr. Jackson was Tim and Angelina's account manager. He knew them very well and they had been loyal customers of the bank for many years.

"Hello," Mr. Jackson answered.

"Good afternoon, Mr. Jackson. This is Tim Branch."

"Hello, Mr. Branch. What can I do for you today?"

"Mr. Jackson, I just realized that an amount of 1.5 million dollars was transferred from my bank account today to a bank in the Philippines."

"Yes, Mr. Branch. Your wife Angelina authorized the transaction and $450.000.00 scheduled to be transferred today."

"I did not authorize this transaction, Mr. Jackson."

"Well, it's already too late for me to do anything with the 1.5 million dollars which have already left our bank. Your wife Angelina is an authorized signatory to the account and there is nothing illegal with this. Therefore, the transaction was legitimate. But, what I can do for you though is put a hold on the pending transaction of the $450,000.00, which is on schedule to be completed by the end of the day pending investigation by the bank."

"Thanks Mr. Jackson."

"You are welcome."

"Are you saying that there's nothing I can do legally regarding the 1.5 million dollars that has been transferred?"

"Unless you are legally divorced from her before she made this transaction, you may bring a legal action against her. But you have to take it up to the courts. That is not something we handle here."

"We are separated. She moved away from our marital residence long ago and filed an order of protection against me and was awarded a monthly payment for child support."

"But you are still, legally married, although unofficially separated. Your money is considered hers, just as hers is considered yours. But after my investigation is successfully completed, depending on the outcome, you can remove her as a signatory on all your accounts. But as it stands right now, she can make any monetary transaction from your joint accounts as she wishes. But as stated earlier, I have put a stop to the pending transaction and placed a hold on your account, blocking further transactions on all your accounts."

"Thank you, Mr. Jackson."

Tim got the information he needed, but not the answer he wanted. He was happy that the bank would put a hold on their accounts, preventing them from making any transactions. His wife could not steal any more money from his accounts. He was only concerned now for the well-being of his son and how and when to get the divorce process started.

He picked up his phone and called his attorney, Marten Lorluk.

"Hello," Mr. Lorluk answered.

"Hello Mr. Lorluk, this Tim Branch."

"Hello, Tim. How are you doing today?"

"Mr. Lorluk, I need to file for divorce."

"Okay, Mr. Branch. I'm sorry to hear that you are ending your marriage, but I'll be glad to handle that transaction for you. But I'll be out of town for a short while. I'll return to work early Monday morning. Is Monday 11.00 a.m. a good time for us to meet?"

"Sure."

"Alright Mr. Branch. I hope to see you then. We can discuss your situation in details and proceed accordingly."

"Thanks Mr. Lorluk."

The moment Tim finished his conversation with Mr. Lorluk, a lady client Juliana Starr walked into the office. She was received by Monica, Tim's secretary. Monica informed him of the client.

"Tim, can you see a client right now?"

"Yes, send her in please."

Juliana walked into Mr. Branch's office. Juliana was a young college graduate. She had majored in business. She wanted to get some business advice from Mr. Branch.

Tim engaged mostly in the accounting and consulting business. It contributed to less than one percent of his gross income. The income derived from such a transaction helped pay for the light and cleaning expense.

As Juliana walked in, Tim looked up. He wanted to see who was coming in. It was a beautiful lady, about 5 ft. 5 inches tall, weighing around 120 pounds. She wore a white skirt and a pink blouse that was not fully buttoned. Her nipples were invisibly visible. Her half exposed breasts were full. Tim wasn't sure if she had ever been to his office in the past. She lived close by, he thought. He stood up to greet the young lady.

"Good afternoon. I'm Tim Branch."

"Good afternoon, I'm Juliana," she said, extending her hand to meet Tim's. They shook hands.

"You can have a seat," Tim said, pointing to the chair in front of him.

"Oh thanks," she said, as she sat down.

"Alright. I understand you intend to buy a new business here in New York."

"Yes. That's correct. The current owners agreed to two million dollar offer I made."

She opened her handbag and brought out an envelope. An eight-and-a-half by eleven brown envelope. She opened it and took out the proposed sale agreement.

Tim took the proposal from her and read it to some point and looked up.

"How are you going to finance this?"

"I'll pay it off in cash."

Ms. Starr was probably a young aspiring entrepreneur. She may have inherited some kind of wealth somehow.

"What got you interested in a business like this, Ms. Starr?"

"You can call me Pamela. I prefer to be called Pamela. I like a business that I can work on as well as have time to spend for myself too. That's why I chose a business of this nature."

"I know of someone who is in the same business you are trying to get into. I happen to be his adviser as well. I gotta tell you, she is doing really great."

"I'm sure she is, and I'm excited to get into it."

The seller said they intend to sell as soon as they can find a qualified buyer; they would then be ready to wrap it up now."

"Are a few weeks alright? Like, one or two weeks?"

"I'm okay with it." She gave him the counter offer for the sellers.

"Where will you be heading to after this?"

"I'll be heading to the hotel on Fifth Avenue."

"I'll contact the sellers tomorrow. As a matter of fact, I'll give them a call this evening before I leave to arrange for a time and date for the transaction, and I'll inform you by phone. How long are you going to be there at the hotel?"

"I intend to fly down to Nevada late tomorrow evening, but I'll be back as soon as I hear from you about the transaction. When you schedule the appointment, please make it for the morning."

"Oh sure." Tim breathed in and out. He felt a little nervous. He hadn't approached a woman in a long time since he had gotten married until he was sure he'd end his marriage with Angelina.

"You are pretty."

"Uh, thanks."

"Would you like to hang out tonight before heading to Nevada?"

She looked surprised and smiled softly. "Is this like a part of the business?"

"No, not at all. This is something I want to do for you."

"I'd love it."

She got up. Tim thought she was going to walk out, but instead, she shook his hand once more.

"When do you want me to be ready?"

"I can drive down there around 8.45, if that's fine."

"I'll be waiting for you then."

She made her way outside and left the office.

Tim watched her while she was walking away. He got a good look at her buttocks.

"Damn!" He could not help but exclaim, "This indeed is better than I imagined", as he looked at her with lustful eyes.

Twenty seven.

Angelina and Brian woke up together that afternoon. She was happy with the verdict. She was enjoying her newfound protection and income. With this income coming in, she didn't have to work any time soon. She would sit home and relax as the monthly payment came in from the family court. They had been living together for almost five months now.

This was exactly the kind of life Brian wanted. He'd been on and off different jobs. On each job he held previously, he had been fired for drug use or possession. He didn't let Angelina know of his drug habits. He currently had a girlfriend, Bridget, who used drugs just as much as he did. They both got high together. Angelina didn't know about his girlfriend and Brian wouldn't want him to because now he could live off her.

It was getting close to evening. The sun had just gone down. It was around 6.30 p.m. Angelina and Brian felt like going outside. They wanted to leave the house for a while.

"Honey?"

"Yes baby?"

"Why don't we get dressed and go outside for a while?"

"Okay. I will. I was thinking about it myself."

"Do you have any place in mind?"

"I think the bar by the seaside will be a perfect place for the evening."

"You mean the Baterra Tavern?"

"Yes. I love the setup up of the outer space."

"Alright baby, I'll be ready in a bit."

Brian went into the shower and shaved off his tiny beard. He came out and put on his clothes, getting ready. He stood in the middle of the living room, glancing at the television. He called out to Angelina.

"Honey, I'm ready."

"Okay honey. I'm getting dressed. I'm almost done. I just gotta put on my makeup and we'll be ready to go."

"Take your time honey. There's no rush. It's open twenty-fours."

Angelina had finished putting on her make ups and dress. She was ready for the night. She looked attractive as always. She walked toward the living room where Brian was waiting and they walked out together for the evening, heading to the bar by the seaside.

They arrived at the bar and sat on the outside by the entrance. Brian loved to drink brandy. The receptionist approached them and he ordered a glass of brandy with ice and lemon juice. Angelina was not a regular drinker. She did not drink alcoholic beverages as much. She ordered a cola with ice. She was a little hungry as well, so she asked for a plate of salmon with rice and carrots. Their order was ready in very little time. There they were, enjoying the evening, wining and dining. Just as Angelina was about to sip her cola, her phone rang. It was inside her handbag. She quickly unzipped the handbag, took the phone out, and answered the call.

"Hello?"

"Hello Angelina, this is Sunny."

"Hi Sunny."

"I'm fine. I just wanna let you know that your house is ready. You can move in at any time."

"Oh great. I actually dreamed about it last night and even right now."

"Oh! What a coincidence!"

Angelina's house in Manila was now complete with all amenities – Jacuzzi, swimming pool, tennis, basketball courts, etc.

"When do you intend to occupy it?"

"You called at the right time. I can schedule my visit to Manila by the end of the week."

"Okay, Angie. Just let me know when."

"Sure."

Brian sat beside her as she conversed with Sunny, not particularly paying attention to the conversation. He was busy making love to his brandy. Out of curiosity, he wanted to know who she was talking to so excitedly.

"Honey, who's that? You sounded so excited. That's gotta be someone important."

"It's my brother in Manila."

"Yea?"

"Yea. He just called to let me know that my house is completed."

"Congratulations! Baby, you are charming."

Angie smiled while Brian reached over for her cheek and kissed her softly.

"When will you be travelling to see the house?"

"This will be a very good time to go there. I'm all excited about it, and it's time my son goes to stay with his father for a while."

Tim usually got to keep his son for thirty days after which he returned him back to his mother, in accordance with the court order.

"Oh that's right. You won't have the burden of travelling with a child and I'll be here taking care of the house."

"That's right. I know you'll take care of things till I get back."

Brian had something else in mind, of which Angelina was unaware of.

It had been a beautiful night for them; done with eating and drinking, they decided to head back home. She signaled to the waitress to know that they were ready to leave and she came over to them.

"Can I have my bill please?"

The waiter wrote the check and handed it to Brian. Angelina took the check from Brian. She reached toward her wallet, brought out her debit card, and handed it over to the waiter. The waitress swiped the credit card for processing. The transaction was approved. Angelina left a $35.00 cash tip for the waitress at the table, and then made their way out of the restaurant.

Twenty-eight

Ready to travel to the Philippines to see her newly built house, Angelina called the airlines to book a flight to Manila.

"Reservations.", the receptionist answered.

"I'd like to book a flight to Manila for Saturday morning."

"Will it be a round trip?"

"Yes."

"Okay. When would you like to return?"

"Any day next week will be fine, preferably on the weekend."

"Hold on please, while I check for flight availability."

Angelina waited while the attendant looked for available dates. She found some dates but had additional questions for her.

"How long do you intend to stay?"

"Thirty days."

"I have a flight that will leave New York for Manila on Friday the 1st and another returning from Manila to

New York on Monday, the 31st. Would you want me to reserve a seat for you?"

"Yes please."

"Will that be economy or business class?"

"Business class."

"The cost for a round trip on the 31st is $3647.00. Would you like to reserve a seat?"

"Yes please."

"How do you intend to pay for this?"

"With a debit card."

"I'm ready when you are."

She gave the agent the debit card information over the phone. She processed the card and the booking was approved.

"Thank you, Mrs. Branch. I have sent the confirmation and the electronic ticket to your email. You can print it out when you are ready to travel."

"Thank you."

She hung up. She waited for about five minutes and called Sunny in Manila.

"Hello?"

"I have just completed booking my flight to Manila."

"Good. When are you coming?"

"I will leave New York on Friday to arrive in Manila the next morning at 6.30 a.m. your time."

"How long do you intend to stay here?"

"Thirty days. I'll leave on the 31st."

"Just one month? Isn't that too short? I think you should book an open ticket in case you decide to stay longer to enjoy your house. After all, this is your first trip to the Philippines since you left for America."

An open ticket allows travelers to stay as long as they wish to and return when they want to without paying additional fee or penalty. Angelina thought about it for a while. She felt that was a good idea.

"Yes Sunny. I think I'm going to do that. As soon as we are done talking, I will call the airline to make the needed changes to an open ticket."

"Okay Angie. I hope to see you soon. I'll be at the airport on Friday morning waiting for your arrival."

"See you then, brother."

They hung up. Angelina immediately called the airline to make the changes as suggested by Sunny.

"Reservations?"

"I'm Mrs. Branch. I made a reservation travelling from New York to Manila and would like to make some adjustments. The reservation number is 657CVZNYMNMNNY."

The agent ran the number on the data board and her information came up on the screen.

"What changes would you like to make?"

"I'll need to make it an open ticket."

"No problem Mrs. Branch. There will an additional charge of $350.00 to make this change and this will be added to your debit card. Do you want me to proceed?"

"Go ahead."

"Okay Mrs. Branch, the extra $350.00 has been billed to your card. You now have an open ticket. Would you like me to make a hotel accommodation for you as well?"

"No thanks. I just built a new house in Manila."

"Great. You are all set. Enjoy your new house."

"Thank you."

Angie successfully completed this transaction. She was happy with the outcome. Everything was going her way as planned. She walked to the bedroom where Brian was sitting getting ready to doze off, but she got his attention.

"The reservation is complete. I will be leaving on Friday."

"When will you be coming back?"

"It depends. But you know that I can't stay too long?"

"Why not, if you have to?"

"Because of my son."

"Oh yeah. I almost forgot about that."

"He has to go to his father."

"I'll make sure that I drop him off by your husband after taking you to the airport."

"My ex-husband."

"Sorry, your ex-husband. I should have known better."

"Are you trying to take me back to him?" she said in jest.

"Hell no. I hate it when I hear of him."

"Me too. We have nothing in common besides the baby."

"Why don't you divorce him?"

"I'm not ready yet."

Brian looked at her. He went close to her and wrapped his hands around her.

"And what are you waiting for?"

"If I divorce him, it would mean that we have to divide everything in half. I want the money all to myself."

"You are right baby. Perhaps it's better if he is dead."

"That's a good idea. After all, in marriage, as the saying goes, it's until death do us part."

"I love you baby. I can take care of that for you."

"How?"

"Put him down. I'll kill him."

She paused for a while and began to rub his chest. Her son was there listening, but they did not know that he was there. He had hidden behind the chair.

"I don't wanna lose now honey."

"Baby, you don't to have to worry about that. I won't get caught. I'll have someone else make the hit."

Tim Jr. suddenly sneezed.

She pushed Brian away a little bit and shouted

"Oh shit, he's here?"

"Honey, don't worry about it. I don't think he heard or understood what we said."

"Yes. Even if he heard us, he probably didn't understand what we were talking about."

She now turned her attention to him.

"Junior?"

"Yes mom?"

"What are you doing?"

"Playing with my toys."

She walked over to him, picked him up and joined him.

Twenty-nine

Tim arrived at the hotel on a private limousine. Pamela was already waiting for him at the reception. Tim walked into the hotel and saw Pamela standing.

She was dressed in a tight open blouse and a mini skirt , showing off her tender legs on spiky high heels. Her lips were painted red. Her hair was dark-colored, sort of brown. Tim walked up to her and extended his hand. She grabbed his hand and they began to the limousine.

The vehicle was parked in front of the hotel. As they walked closer to it, Tim pointed at the vehicle.

"That's our ride right here."

The driver opened the rear door for them. Tim held the door as Pamela went in and sat down. He got into the vehicle himself and sat closer to her. Shortly after, the chauffeur drove off slowly.

"We're not going too far. The restaurant is about fifteen blocks from here," Tim said.

"Yea, a friend of mine told me about the place, but I haven't been there before."

"It's a very beautiful place to hang out, and I'm sure you will like it."

They arrived at the hotel, walked inside and sat down.

"It looks good. I like the set up."

While they sat conversing, a waitress showed up and handed them the menu. They glanced at it and started picking out their choices.

"May I have a glass of wine with a little ice in it for now?" Pamela requested.

"It seems we have the same choices. I'll have the same thing as her."

The waitress walked away to get their orders and Tim continued.

"Where did you learn to drink red wine?"

"It's an alcoholic beverage made from grapes without the addition of sugars. I learned it is good for the heart."

"I read about it in the journal of medicine myself. You are right. It is good for the heart."

"I'm sure."

"The business you intend to go into is a lucrative one. I am sure you will do well."

"My parents are successful business people. It is in our genes. As a journalist, I was able build up my career. I made millions and saved a lot."

"What a lucky girl you are!" You got kids?"

"Not yet. Never been married."

"Boyfriend, perhaps?"

"I left him a long time ago. What about you?"

"My wife abandoned me."

"How long has it been?"

"More than a year ago."

"How have you stayed so long without a woman?"

"Been pretty much occupied with my work. When you are self-employed, it's tough. Although you have workers, you still gotta put in a lot of hours. They can't make decisions without you."

"I guess that's why some of the self-employed people are so successful."

"I guess so, but it's not so easy. The good thing about it is that it allows you time to (a) do whatever you want to do, (b) work when you want to and (c) leave when you want to."

The waitress returned with the order and placed it on their table. They picked up the glass of wine.

"Cheers!" they said.

"Are you thinking about divorce?"

"It's already on its way. My attorney is out on vacation and hope to get it started as soon as he returns. How did you guess so correctly?"

"Looking at you, it's not difficult to imagine what you can do. With your shy beautiful smile, you don't seem to be that kind of a person who would linger so long without a woman."

"Not just that. It's just that when you have a baby involved, you're always careful when making decisions, especially a quick one that can affect your lives. I just hate that I didn't act fast enough to delete her name from my bank account. That has cost me a million and a half that she transferred out of my bank account to Manila."

"You can call yourself lucky. My friend got away with half of her husband's wealth – 1.2 billion in settlement.

"I can agree with you. That's one of the reasons I was hoping to get an out-of-court settlement. She has made other attempts to transfer a couple of millions, but I was able to catch up with that on time."

"How?"

"I got the bank to put a hold on the accounts that she had access to. They stopped the other transfers on time before it left the bank."

"You mentioned earlier that the money was wired to Manila. Why Manila? Do you know?"

"She's from the Philippines. Manila is the capital city of the Philippines."

"Most foreigners are like that. They're not about true love, especially when they get the green card. I heard about so many stories like that."

"This was a great mistake on my side. I was deceived. I wish I could have known better or had listened to others. What about you? Are you considering getting back with your boyfriend?"

"Hell, no! I still love him, but we can never get back together again. It ain't gonna work and it ain't gonna happen, not even if he wants to. I've given up the hurtful feelings a long time ago."

"That's great. Feeling hurt is not such a good thing. I know exactly how you feel. That's why I am sort of relieved now in many ways. But let's talk about something else. I enjoyed listening to you on the weather channel."

"Thank you. How did you know I'm the one?"

"I just guessed. Your name sounded so familiar. When I first met you, I knew I had seen or heard you somewhere, but I wasn't exactly sure."

"What a small world! Journalism is good, but I prefer indoor work. In journalism, you are always exposed."

"I guess you like attention."

"I can say I do, but I prefer indoor games."

"Do you wish to continue in your journalism career after you purchase your business?"

"Yes, but I'm going to let my associates handle most the work on my behalf."

"You are very smart lady."

"Most men don't always think that way. Do I take it as a compliment?"

"More than a compliment?"

Tim sipped a little and held the glass in his hand. Pamela sipped a little from the straw and put the glass back on the table. They looked into each other's eyes. Tim winked his eyes and Pamela smiled softly.

"You are fun to be with, Tim Branch."

"You are fun to be with, Pamela Starr."

Thirty

Angelina was ready to travel to Manila to see and spend some time in her new home. She got dressed and was ready to go the airport.

"Honey, are you ready?" Angelina said.

"Yes, honey. I'm ready whenever you are."

"Oh, wait a minute. I wanna see what the baby is doing."

Angelina saw where her son was waiting and said to him, "Okay Junior, let's go."

"Okay mom."

"Did you bring all your toys with you?"

"Yes mom."

Tim Jr. had packed up all his toys, including one of the pipes Brian used to get high on drugs. Junior, of course, had no idea what it was, but he enjoyed playing with it. Occasionally, he would put some water into the pipe hole and blow bubbles out of it. Angelina didn't know that Brian was a drug addict. She also did not know that the pipe was in her son's toy bag.

Brian picked up all of Angelina's luggage and headed outside to the vehicle. He put them in the trunk and drove off to the airport. But first, they had to drop off Junior at his father's house. They drove closer to the house and parked, waiting for Tim to pick up his son. Junior got out of the car and waited for his father while Angelina and Brian stayed in the vehicle, waiting until Junior was picked up by his father. Tim walked up to Junior, held him by the hand, and walked away back to his house.

"Alright, he got him. Let's go. We are running late," Angelina said.

"Alright."

Brian sped away. They were heading to the airport. Angelina called Sunny.

"Hello."

"I'll be boarding the plane in less than 30 minutes and will arrive in Manila as scheduled."

"I'll be at the airport, waiting for you."

"See you then."

Angelina and Brian arrived at the JFK International Airport Departures section. They came to the terminal. Sunny pulled up and quickly took out her luggage from the trunk, hauled them inside the airport, and came back outside. They hugged and kissed each other.

"Bye honey, travel safe."

"Bye now, take care of yourself."

"I will."

Angie walked into the terminal, boarded the plane and departed to Philippines while Brian drove away and headed home. While driving, his cell phone rang and he answered.

"Hello!"

"Where are you?" Bridget, his girlfriend asked. They had broken up when he had lost his job, but got back together after he started dating Angelina. They had an open relationship, but the crack cocaine kept them inseparable. Bridget had never held a job before.

"I'm on the way, coming back from the airport."

"And where will you be?"

"I'll be at the smoke shop waiting for you."

"I should be there within an hour."

"Hurry the fuck up."

One hour later, Brian arrived at the smoke shop. There was Bridget, waiting outside, shivering. It was quite cold out there and she immediately got into the vehicle. Brian pulled up in front of the shop and parked. He got out of the vehicle while she waited and went into the shop. He purchased some smoke pipes and needles used to inject crack inside the body, went back into the car, and drove three blocks down. The drug dealer came out to meet them. He knew them very well. They were his regular customers and he knew exactly what they wanted. Brian handed the cash to him and received the cocaine, dust and crack from him. He drove away quickly, headed back to Angelina's apartment.

They arrived at Angelina's apartment and began smoking and injecting drugs. They had good sex all day and as often as they could.

Thirty one

When Angelina left Tim's residence, she had fired Lissandra, their house keeper. Lissandra had given Tim her contact information before she left.

Tim called Lissandra.

"Hello sir."

"Hello Lissandra, how are you doing today?"

"I'm fine, thank you."

"Have you found another employment?"

"Nothing yet, but I am still looking."

"Do you mind taking care of my son?"

"No sir. I'd love to."

"If you can come over tonight, it will be great!"

"I'm on my way."

She got dressed very quickly, took the bus and headed over to Tim's residence. She arrived at the residence in less than one hour and rang the bell. Tim let her in.

"Thanks for coming back," Tim said, and they shook hands.

"Thanks for hiring me back sir."

"As per court order, my son will be staying with me for thirty days and will be returned to his mother thereafter. My contract with you will be for thirty days every other month. Is that alright with you?"

"Yes. That's fine with me sir."

"What are you expecting for your monthly salary?"

"When your wife Angelina hired me, she and I agreed to $500.00 per week. I can settle for the same."

Tim looked astonished. Angelina had gotten $1000.00 from him every week for her but was paying her only $500.00.

Tim walked away.

"What a mess!" He thought to himself. "I was deceived. My wife was taking $1000.00 from me but paid only $500.00 to the maid. Is that something else I don't know of. This woman is a crook."

He walked out and went to work. Lissandra was now back at her job.

Thirty-two

Angelina arrived at Ninoy Aquino, Manila International Airport, in the Philippines. She exited the airplane, went through the customs check successfully, and walked over to the waiting area of the arrival section. She stopped for a moment with a beautiful smile on her face, looking around, hoping to spot Sunny. He was supposed to be there waiting for her to arrive. But she didn't see him yet. She looked at her watch. It was thirty minutes before the hour. Her plane had arrived thirty minutes before schedule.

She walked back over to the side and sat down. Sitting down, she looked around for Sunny, but he wasn't there yet. More than thirty minutes had passed since she had arrived, and now she thought it wise to call him. She picked up her cell phone and called Sunny.

"Hello?" Sunny answered.

"I have arrived. I'm standing in front of the taxi stand holding a luggage. Can you see me?"

"No. I'm not there yet. My vehicle broke down on the highway. I'm stranded here by the toll bridge waiting for the tow truck."

"Sorry to hear that. What do you suggest I do now?"

"Hang on for a minute please. The tow truck is here. Let me attend to him."

After a while, Sunny returned to the line and continued.

"Okay. You can take a taxi from there and meet me in front of your house."

"Okay. I'll hop on a cab right now. See you soon."

Angie walked across to the taxi line. The next taxi in line pulled up beside her. The driver got out of the taxi cab, opened the trunk, took her bag from her and put it in the trunk of the vehicle, while she got into the taxi.

"Good morning lady. Where would you like to go?" the driver asked.

She reached inside her pocket and took out a piece of paper where she wrote down the address of her house and handed it to the taxi driver. The driver read the address. He was familiar with the address. He looked at Angelina and handed the paper back to her.

"You know how to get there?"

"Yes ma'am. I've been driving for years. I know every place in Manila."

The driver adjusted his rearview mirror, started the engine, and drove off.

Sunny called Angelina and she picked up.

"Hello?"

"I'm in front of your building. I'll be standing outside, waiting for you."

"Okay, I'm in the taxi now. We are on the way."

Thirty-three.

Angelina arrived at her new house. The driver got out and walked over to the back to open the trunk and unpack the luggage. She got out of the cab and paid him a hundred dollars. The driver stared at the notes. It was American currency.

"You are an American," the driver said.

"Yes, but I was born here. I moved to the United States many years ago."

"Welcome home."

"Thank you."

"Do you want your change?"

"Keep the change."

"Thanks ma'am."

Sunny was supposed to be standing in front the building, but did not approach the taxi cab yet. Angelina looked around for him but did not see him. The driver was still standing by, waiting for her to go inside the building before he drove away. But she looked rather astonished, still standing around, seemingly confused. The driver took notice of this and hung around. She walked toward the building. It was a big mansion, beautiful by appearance, and the security guard was sitting inside the security gate. She saw a man standing by, but said nothing to the man. She took out her cell phone and dialed Sunny. His phone rang, but it went straight to his voicemail. She did not leave a message. She walked toward the taxi driver.

"Driver, I see that you haven't left yet. Can you still hang around for a little while?"

"Yes man. No problem."

She walked toward the security gate to the security guard. The security guard slid the glass open to address her.

"Good afternoon," she said to the guard.

"Yes ma'am, may I help you?"

"Can you tell me where Sunny is?"

"There's no such person here as Sunny."

"Oh! Maybe you know him by another name, but he is the contractor who built this house for me."

The guard looked at her as if she were crazy or retarded and stood up.

"Did you just say he built this house for you?"

"Yes. This is my house."

"Ma'am, you are in the wrong place. This is Ligaya Isagani's residence. I have been working for this family for over three years."

Angelina was shocked. She couldn't believe her ears. She hadn't seen Sunny since she arrived in Manila.

"No, that can't be."

"Ma'am, are you alright? You need to get out of here right now before I get the police to arrest you."

He picked up a long double barrel gun, cocked it, pointed it at her and yelled, "Get out of here now. Get out."

He fired a warning shot in the air. Angelina reeled back and started walking away very quickly toward the waiting taxi cab. The man standing outside where Sunny was supposed to have been waiting for her wearing a black suit approached her and said, "Hello ma'am."

"Hello."

"Who are you looking for?"

"Sunny"

"Sunny Homobono?"

"Yes. Sunny Homobono."

"I'm waiting for him too. He's on his way and should be arriving shortly. We spoke about an hour ago and he's with a client at another location. He should be here shortly."

"Are you waiting for him as well?"

"Yes. He built this house for me and I am waiting to take a tour of the place."

"Do you mean this house is yours?"

"Yes. I made a down payment of $500,000.00 on the property."

Angelina stood silent, in shock and disbelief. She stood silent for a while.

"No, he couldn't possibly sell this house to you. I paid $1.5 million dollars for this property. It was built for me."

The man wouldn't believe her. He laughed. He thought she was just crazy.

"Are you sure about what you are saying?"

"Yes. He is my younger brother."

The man took out his phone from his bag. He checked the time. It was long past the hour Sunny told him he would be getting there. He dialed his number and put the phone on the speaker mode. His phone rang, but a recorded message came on: This phone is not accepting incoming calls at this time.

Angelina heard the recording from the man's speaker phone. She then decided it was about time she called him as well. She took out her phone and dialed the number. She got the same recorded message as the man.

"This phone is not accepting incoming calls at this time."

The man walked with Angelina to the waiting taxi driver.

"Driver?"

"Yes, man."

"I recall you telling me that you know every place in Manila, right?"

"Yes ma'am."

"Do you know who owns this house?"

"Yes. This house belongs to Ligaya Isagani, a very wealthy woman. She lives here with her family."

Angelina and the man were beginning to realize that it was a sham. They had been duped by Sunny

Homobono. They looked at each other with deep disappointment.

"We have been deceived!" Both of them were close to tears.

"I will kill him if he doesn't return my money," Angelina said.

"I'll help you. I'm with you on that. I am a Filipino and will never let this happen to me here."

Angelina was incredibly upset about this whole thing. She remembered the bank where she transferred the $1.5 million dollars to.

"Driver, take us to the Philippine National Bank. Do you want the address?"

"No ma'am. I know the address. It is located on Aduana Street, near Arzobispo St, Intramuros, about twenty miles from here. It is a forty-five-minute drive. That will cost one hundred and fifty American dollars."

Both Angelina and Liberato, the other person who was duped, entered the taxi cab.

"No problem. Go ahead. Fast," Angelina said.

"Yes ma'am."

The driver drove off.

Thirty-four.

Angelina and Liberato arrived at the Philippine National Bank. They walked in straight to the receptionist and were warmly received.

"Welcome to the Philippine National Bank."

Angelina opened her bag immediately and brought out a piece of paper, about eight-and-half-by-eleven in size. It contained all the information regarding the money transfer to Sunny's account. She handed the piece of paper to the receptionist and said, "On June 3rd, I transferred $1.5 million dollars to this account for Sunny Homobono for the construction of a new house here in Manila. I live in the United States of America. I need to reconfirm that this money was deposited on this account as per this document."

The receptionist looked at the document given to her by Angelina.

"Okay, give me a minute while I look it up."

The receptionist entered the account information in her data system. She saw that the money was received by the bank but was immediately transferred to a bank in Nigeria. After the transfer, the account was closed at the request of the customer.

"I see that the money was received by this bank on June 24th. On June 25th, the money was transferred to Nigeria, and the account was consequently closed by the bank at the request of the account holder. This is the only information I can give you. Is there anything else I can help you with?"

"No."

"Thanks for using Philippine National Bank."

Without another word, Angelina walked out of the bank with Liberato and got into the waiting cab.

"Driver, take us to the Marriko hotel. I am sure you know where it is, right?"

"Yes ma'am. It's about 15 minutes from here. The cost will be a hundred America dollars, okay?"

"Go ahead."

The driver was off to the hotel. While they were on their way to the hotel, they began conversation.

"I will never let this happen. It's my money or his life," said Liberato.

"You are right. My own brother cannot do this to me and expect to get away with it. He thought I am still the same girl he knew before. I'll kill him."

"How do want to handle this?"

"By any means possible."

"I know a hit man here in Manila. I also have a good connection with the police. In Manila, everything is about money. First, I'll have to get the police to look for him. If that fails, I'll have a hitman deal with him."

"That's right."

"Alright Mrs. Branch, leave this to me. I'll handle it."

They arrived at the hotel; the driver pulled up to the drop-off area. Angelina got out of the cab first and Liberato followed suit. The driver popped open the trunk and Liberato helped unload Angelina's luggage and went back into the taxi cab. He decided to head back home. She paid $300.00 in total to the driver, which included the tip. He accepted the money cheerfully.

"Thank you. Here's my business card. Call me when you need a taxi."

"I will."

"Good night Mrs. Branch. I'll be back tomorrow to meet you. We can sit down privately and discuss how to handle this," said Liberato.

"Good night."

She went upstairs to her hotel room while the driver drove away with Liberato.

Thirty-five.

Lissandra was getting ready to take Tim Junior out to the park when she saw him playing with some toys, one of which looked like a pipe. She came closer to him and looked at the pipe to be certain of what she thought she saw.

"Junior, let me have this."

"No no no," Junior said and began to move away slowly from her. She followed him as he began to run around in the house as if she was playing with him, laughing and chasing him around. He hid the pipe under the chair away from her. Lissandra pretended as if she did not see it.

"Come and get it," Junior said, extending his hand toward her with his fist tightened.

"Okay, give it to me."

He opened his hands in front of her.

"Take it". But there was nothing in his hands to be taken. He laughed, under the impression that he was deceiving her. Lissandra played along.

She picked him up, bent down, and quickly took the pipe from under the chair, without Junior noticing anything. She put the pipe in her pocket and put him to sleep with a lullaby.

She looked very closely at the pipe. It didn't seem like a regular toy to her. It looked like the pipes drug addicts use to smoke heroin, crack, or cocaine or some other life-threatening addictives.

"How did he get this?" she marveled. She couldn't possibly think of how a pipe used for getting high could wind up in the hands of a toddler.

"His father has to see this," she said to herself and sat down.

Tim incidentally dropped by the house that afternoon during his lunch break. He wanted to check on his son and Lissandra. They weren't expecting to see him at that time. He opened the door and walked in. Lissandra turned around and greeted him.

"Good afternoon sir."

"Good afternoon. How are you guys doing?"

"Fine, sir."

"Where is Junior?"

"He just woke up. He's in there in his room, playing."

He walked toward his son's room. Junior saw him and ran up to him shouting, "Daddy, daddy, daddy! Daddy, are you back?"

"Yes son, but not for long. I will be leaving in a minute. I just dropped by to make sure you're alright."

"I'm doing fine."

"Oh great!"

"Daddy!"

"Yes, son."

"Are you going to take me back to mommy?"

"Not today. In a couple of days, you'll be going back to her."

"No. I don't wanna go back there."

"Why not?"

"'Cause I wanna stay with you. I don't like mommy's friend. I wanna stay with you."

"No, son. Don't say that. She's your mommy."

"Her friend smokes a lot of cigarettes when mommy is not there. It makes me sick."

"Only when mommy is not there?"

"Yea."

"We will talk about this later when I come back. I just dropped by to check on you. Right now, I gotta get back to work now."

"Okay daddy. Bye. Don't forget to buy me Elmo."

"I won't forget."

Tim began walking outside toward his car, but Lissandra followed him behind.

"Look what I found in Junior's hands." She handed the pipe to him. He looked at it and was astonished.

"From my son?"

"Yes. I saw him playing with it earlier this morning, and when I saw it, I wanted to take it away from him, but he ran and hid it under the chair. He thought I didn't see it. But I took it away from him."

"Hmm. This looks like an object used by drug addicts in their drug habit."

"Yes. That's exactly what it is used for. I have a brother who is a drug user, so I'm familiar with an instrument like this."

Junior went back to the chair where he hid the toy and knelt down beside it. He looked up to check if someone was looking at him, and they were not looking at him. He lifted up the cushion and turned around again to make sure nobody was watching him. He looked under the chair for the pipe but did not see it. He thought he was looking at the wrong place. He crawled over to the chair next to the one he hid the pipe and stood up, looking at Tim and Lissandra; but they were facing the other way. He lifted up the cushion and did not see the pipe. He started crying.

"Daddy, I can't find my toy anymore. I put it under the chair and now it's not there."

"Stop crying, son. Is this what you are looking for?" He showed the pipe to him.

"Yes. It's mine."

"I know it's yours, but you can't have it back because it is not good for you. I'll buy you another one okay?"

"Okay."

"Where did you get this from?"

"When mommy was not home, her friend was using it to smoke his cigarettes. When he fell asleep in the couch, I took it and hid it with my other toys."

Tim had on him a small recording device. He recorded everything his son said. He had heard enough.

"Thanks, Lissandra."

"You're welcome, sir."

He went into his bedroom, kept the pipe in a secure place, and went away to work.

Thirty-six

The next morning, Liberato came back to the hotel to visit Angelina, as planned. He came with two other people, Benjie Bayani and Marife Killar. He had a plan in mind about how he intended to handle the situation with Sunny. They walked upstairs to her hotel room and she opened the door to receive them.

"Good morning Angelina."

"Good morning Liberato."

"This is Mr. Benjie Bayani and Ms. Marife Killar."

"Welcome guys."

"Thank you," the two of them replied.

"I have made a lot of inquiries about Sunny Homobono and found that he is a notorious guy and is very dangerous. Even the police here are afraid of him. He does not operate alone. Benjie Bayani and Marife Killar are hit men. They can kill you in a minute if you don't cooperate with them. I have hired them to help us recover our money from Sunny."

Bayani and Killar stood silent while Liberato introduced them to Angelina. After he finished, Killar spoke immediately.

"What do you want us to do for you?"

"I want my money back from Sunny," Angelina replied.

"Okay ma'am. That's not a problem at all," Bayani added.

"What if he spent the money and has nothing to give us? What do you want us to do with him then?" Killar said.

"Kill him. I want him dead. I have no sympathy for him now. He robbed me. I work hard for my money."

"I agree with you. I'm with you. You can't steal that amount of money from someone, especially a relative, and expect to get away with it. Not these days."

"We get $20,000.00 for jobs like this. Ten thousand down and the other ten thousand upon completion," Bayani said.

"I agree. How quickly can this be done?" she asked.

"As fast as you wish. Almost immediately. You'll get your money back from him or he's dead."

"I expect to leave for New York soon, but I'd like to see the end of this before I leave."

Angelina reached inside her bag and handed $20,000 cash to Bayani, and he handed it over to Killar. She sat down and began counting it.

While Killar counted the money, Bayani began preparing to act on the contract to recover the money for Angelina and Liberato. He took out his cell phone from his pocket and made a phone call. The phone rang more than six times but there was no answer. He stood silent for less than three seconds. He was calling Sunny.

"He's not picking up. Bastard! You're dead," he said and hung up.

In less than ten seconds after Bayani hung up, there was a knock on the door.

Killar was busy counting the money. Liberato sat still. Bayani was standing, leaning against the side wall. Angelina went to the door and looked through the peephole. She saw two police officers standing in front of the door with their guns drawn. She looked furious. Reeling backward, she checked for a way to exit, but there was no way. She looked at everybody in the room, but no one said anything.

"Open the door. Open the door now," one of the police officers shouted.

"Who are you looking for?" Angelina asked.

"Open the fucking door before we kick it down. This is the police."

She looked at Liberato, Killar, and Bayani. They were all frightened.

She quietly opened the door and the cops walked in, pointing their guns toward her. One of the policemen said, "Turn around. Raise your hands against the wall."

She did as instructed. One of the policemen frisked her, while the other brought out the handcuffs.

"Put your hands behind your back," the officer commanded her. He handcuffed her and began to lead her out of the room.

"What have I done? What's going on?"

"You'll know when we get to the police station."

Liberato, Bayani, and Killar followed her as she was led out to the police car.

She was put at the back of the vehicle and driven to the precinct.

When they arrived at the police station, the officers took her inside the booking area.

"Good afternoon Captain," the officer greeted the Chief.

"Good afternoon."

"This woman has been brought here today because she was plotting to kill somebody by name of Sunny Homobono. She is from America."

"Who? Me? I wasn't plotting to kill anyone."

"Shut up woman," one of the officers shouted. He hit her on the upper back, not with a lot of force but mildly, enough to get her to keep quiet.

"You are not in America. You don't talk when the captain is talking." She kept quiet.

"If you are not plotting to kill someone, why did the police bring you here then?"

"I don't know. I think they have the wrong person. I was in my hotel room with my friends, having a business conference, when they walked in suddenly and arrested me."

"Are you telling me that you were not trying to kill someone here in Manila?"

"Hell, no! I'm not here to kill anyone. I'm only here for a short visit. You have no evidence to back up your claim. Show me the evidence."

Immediately after she had finished making this statement, she heard some noise. She looked behind and saw Liberato, Killar and Bayani walking in. They came and sat down behind where she was standing.

"Yes, here are my friends. Yes, they are here now," she continued.

Liberato reached inside his bag and brought out a small video recording device and handed it over to the captain. The captain plugged the recorder into a wall outlet and turned it on, facing her. Angelina watched the video. She was sitting in the hotel room with Liberato, Bayani and Killar, plotting how to kill Sunny. The captain turned it off.

"You just lied to me that you are here to take care of some business and not plotting to kill anyone. I am going to charge you with plot to murder and lying to deceive authorities."

The two arresting officers unlocked the handcuff from her hands. She tried to escape again, even with the officers holding her down, but was held back and placed in the holding cell.

"You will remain here until I speak to the intended victim, Mr. Sunny Homobono, to find out how he wishes to proceed with this matter. This can take up to several days."

The officer shut the prison cell and walked away with the key.

"Fuck this shit!" She said and sat down.

Thirty-seven.

Tim Branch called his attorney, Mr. Lorluk, who had just returned from a vacation and was now back on the job.

"Mr. Lorluk?"

"Hello Mr. Lorluk, it's Tim Branch. How are you doing?"

"Hey Tim! I feel great. I just got back and was ready to head back to work."

"How was your trip?"

"Great. It was good to get away from work. I usually do this once in a while. What's up?"

"You are already familiar with the problems I have with my wife."

"Yes. I'm aware of that. Are you ready to divorce now?"

"Yes. I'm finally ready; and I have some evidence that may help me get the sole custody of my child."

"Do you want to have full and sole custody of your child?"

"Yes. Full and sole custody."

"Tim, I'm sure you understand what you are asking for. This is a gray area now. It is a difficult thing for a man to get full and sole custody of a child, unless there is credible and convincing evidence. You may want to ask the judge for joint custody."

"I have good evidence, which I believe is credible and convincing."

"And what is that?"

"I found a pipe most drug addicts use to inhale, inject or smoke crack and cocaine in my son's possession when he was brought over to spend time with me in accordance with the court order."

"You mean an object used to smoke heroin?"

"Yes."

"I'm not sure if that alone will convince a judge to grant sole custody to a father, if there is no evidence of consumption. I'm sure you know your wife will deny having any knowledge of how your son got the object."

"The housekeeper found it in his toy box when he was brought over. She saw him playing with it and took it away from him."

"That sounds like a planted evidence, since it was found in your house."

"You are right. I never thought of it that way."

"But if the judge believes that she is in fact a drug user and your son is exposed to danger, the court may grant your request for sole custody. Nevertheless, we can certainly proceed with the case and ask the court for joint custody. Your assets will be divided in accordance with the law."

"Thanks for the advice. I'll get back to you soon."

"You are welcome."

Having gotten the information he desperately wanted from his lawyer, he thought of his next move. He thought about his friend who worked with the police department. He decided he would talk to him. He picked up his phone and dialed his number. The phone rang and he answered.

"Hello?"

"Hey Shawn, I need your help here."

"Yes, talk to me."

"I found a heroin pipe in my son's toy box when he was brought over to my house by his mother, in compliance with the court order. I'm in the process of filing for divorce. I intend to seek the sole custody of my son."

"Does she use drugs?"

"Not that I know of. I have not observed any such habit from her since we've been together. But since she moved out, she's been living with a man I believe is her boyfriend."

"Brian Steeler."

"Look, I think I may have to contact the Child Protective Services regarding this matter. This is something serious. They may have to pay a visit to their home based on what you just told me. Nevertheless, I will ask for a search warrant to gain access to her home."

"Thanks Shawn."

"Look, you don't have to worry about anything. I'm only doing my job. The police department is here to protect its citizens."

"Thanks Shawn."

Thirty-eight.

Liberato called Sunny. The phone rang and Sunny answered.

"Hello Liberato."

"Hey. Everything has been taken care of. It worked out as planned."

"Where is she now?"

"She's at the police station and is being held in a small detention cell. The captain is waiting for your order."

Liberator was Sunny's partner-in-crime. He was a very smart guy, and he had executed the plan successfully, just as Sunny had wanted. He was eager to know what the next move was.

"Great. Now I want her out of the Philippines immediately, within the next 24 hours."

"Okay sir. That will be taken care of."

"Take $5000.00 out of the money you have and give to the police captain for a job well done. Get her out of the cell and take her straight to the airport. She has an open ticket."

"It will be taken care of immediately."

Liberato got into his vehicle and drove straight to the police station. He arrived in time to meet with the captain.

"I have a message for you captain."

He pulled out a brown envelope from his bag. Inside the envelope was $5000.00 from Sunny to compensate him for a job well done.

"I want her out of the here now. She'll be departing the country tonight."

The captain immediately gave an order to have Angelina released to Liberato. Liberato took out his phone and called the airlines to make sure they had a plane leaving tonight.

"Philippine Airlines, may I help you?"

"When is the next flight leaving from Manila to the United States?"

"Are you the travelling passenger?"

"Yes."'

"Have you made any reservations with us?"'

"No. I intend to travel to New York as quickly as possible."

"I have a flight departing from Manila tonight at 11.30 p.m., which is scheduled to arrive in New York by 4.30 a.m. Do you want me to reserve a seat for you now?"

"No. I don't have my credit card with me right now. I will call you back in a minute to make the reservation."

He hung up immediately. He heard what he had wanted to know. A flight was to depart from Manila to New York that very night. He wanted to make sure of this before Angelina was released.

He walked back inside the station. Angelina was standing there, holding a sandwich in her hand. That was her morning breakfast. She ate it halfway but was unable to finish it. She didn't like the taste. She looked tired, frail and disgusted. She looked up and saw Liberato. The same man Sunny supposedly scammed, although she knew better now. The Sunny she knew was not the same person he was, quiet and humble. He had turned into a big criminal, with corrupt government authorities and gangs protecting him.

She walked outside the police cell to the vehicle parked outside, escorted by Liberato.

"Get in here," Liberato said.

She got into the vehicle and sat down. Liberato slammed the door shut. The vehicle had a locking system that once closed could not be opened from inside. Angelina was confused.

"Where are you taking me to?"

"I'm taking you to the airport by the order of your brother Sunny. He doesn't want you dead because you are his sister."

"I'm his sister?"

"Yes, that's what he told me. You are siblings and grew up together."

"He knows that I'm his sister and he robbed me?"

"I'm not here to take any questions from you. I only answer to Sunny and follow his orders."

"I have been deceived."

"You are lucky to be alive."

"Where is my luggage?"

"In the trunk, with your passport and flight ticket. You have an open ticket."

She paused for a while and sat back. She was being taken to the airport, forced out of her own country. She couldn't believe what was happening to her. Her father and mother were ailing and she wanted to see them.

"Take me to my parents' house instead. I want to see them before I leave."

"Shut the fuck up lady. Did I not tell you that you are departing Manila tonight? Sunny will kill you if you don't get out of town tonight. The police will come and arrest you again and charge you with another crime; you can then spend twenty years in prison here."

It was about 10 p.m. when they arrived at the airport. He unpacked her luggage, opened her handbag, and gave her her passport. He walked her straight to the terminal. The plane was already idling.

"Fuck you!" she said to Liberato.

"You are a motherfucker. Fuck out of here. Americana." Liberato said, laughing at her and waited until the airplane took off with her to New York.

Thirty-nine

Angelina arrived at New York early morning. Brian and Bridget were together at Angelina's apartment, getting high on coke. It was about 4.30 a.m. in the morning when his phone rang. He looked anxious. He wasn't expecting any phone calls at that time of the day. Angelina was away and he was with Bridget. He took a quick snorting of the cocaine and walked slowly over to the phone and answered.

"Hello?"

"Honey, it's me. I'm at the airport. You can come and get me," Angelina said.

"You are at the airport?"

"Yes. Come and get me quickly."

"Okay, but you gotta give some time. I gotta get dressed and then go to the gas station to fill up the tank. It's nearly empty."

"Okay. Hurry."

"Okay." He turned around to Bridget.

"She's back... Hey! You gotta leave."

"Why did she return so early? Why didn't she call before she came?"

"Just put on your fucking clothes man! We gotta get out of here real quick."

Bridget began to get dressed. She didn't need a lot of time, while Brian started cleaning out the room. He vacuumed the living and the bedrooms very fast and sprayed a lot of air fresheners all over the room and cleaned out the bathroom. He opened the windows to let some fresh air to come in. He wanted to make sure that Angelina did not smell any funny odors when she comes in.

He looked around the room to make sure that there was no trace of drugs. He felt confident that the room was free of drugs.

"We gotta get out of here now."

"Let's go," said Bridget.

Brian and Bridget ran down through the stairs quickly and got into the vehicle. He drove off quickly and dropped her off by the crack house and headed straight to the port.

Angelina was standing at the waiting lot, when Brian arrived. He got out of the vehicle and welcomed her with hugs and kisses. He then took her luggage and put it inside the trunk as she went into the car and sat down. He got back into the vehicle and drove off.

"Welcome back, honey."

"Thank you."

"How was your trip?"

"Fine. I had a good time, but had to cut it short."

"You didn't call me before you left."

"My battery was dead, so I decided I'll call you when I get to the airport."

"Why did you cut your trip so short?"

"It was boring."

"I guess, without me."

" Yes. Besides, I finished everything I had to do on time."

They arrived home. They got out of the vehicle and Brian took out the luggage from the trunk. They walked upstairs into their apartment.

She undressed very quickly and took a good shower. She hadn't had a bath since she was held in a detention cell in Manila.

"I miss you honey,"' Brian said.

"I miss you too," she replied.

266

They lay side by side in bed. Brian took his shirt off and got on top of her, between her legs, and started caressing her. Very quickly, he got erect and his heart started beating faster. He began making love to her. She didn't look very happy. She was still thinking about what had happened to her in Manila. She couldn't believe that her brother was capable of doing what he did to her. She laid still while Brian did all the work. He got tired and ejaculated very quickly. He fell asleep almost immediately. She got up, went to the bathroom, rinsed herself and caught up on the sleep she had lost while being detained in Manila.

The next morning, Angelina woke up and wasn't feeling very good. Brian was still deep in his sleep. She went to the kitchen and boiled some hot water for coffee. She sat down at the dining table as she sipped the coffee, while watching television in disgust. Brian walked over to the dining area where she was sitting.

"Good morning honey."

"Good morning."

"You don't look too happy this morning."

"Yes. I'm not feeling too good."

"What's the matter?"

"I feel weak and tired. I have pain all over my body. My teeth and stomach also hurt."

"Are you pregnant?"

"I don't think so. I didn't feel this way even when I was pregnant with my first child. I have never felt like this before."

"I suggest you go see a doctor right away."

"Yes. I think I should do that right away."

Angelina started getting dressed and so did Brian. They were headed to the hospital.

When they arrived at the clinic, she waited at the emergency area with him. A doctor approached them and she walked inside the diagnosis room to be examined.

"You can lie down on your back here," the doctor said.

She laid down on her back on the examination bed. The doctor ran a few checks on her, including her heart rate, but found nothing.

"Everything seems to be alright. I'll have to run a blood test on you to determine what's going on, but I'll need your consent. Do you wish to continue?"

"Yes."

The doctor gave her a consent form and she accepted it from him. She filled it up and gave it back to him.

"The result will be back in three days. I hope to see you then."

"See you then."

She left the examination room and walked back over to the waiting area toward Brian. He saw her approaching and got up. Together, they left the hospital, holding hands.

Three days later, the results came in as scheduled. She went to the hospital and was met by her doctor. The doctor walked her into a private room and sat down. He brought out the test results.

"Hello Mrs., Branch."

"Hello sir."

"How are you feeling today?"

"Not so well. I am getting increasingly weaker."

"Well, I hate to inform you that the results of your test reveals that you have the HIV virus."

"HIV?", she screamed in disbelief.

"Yes. HIV, the virus that causes AIDS."

"How did I possibly contract such a virus?"

"It's commonly spread through sexual encounter with someone who has it – drug addicts and homo and bisexuals alike."

"I have only one partner who I live with, and I'm sure he doesn't have it."

"You don't know that. You don't know who he slept with in the past before he met you."

"Where do I go from here?"

"Well, at this point in time, there is no known cure for the virus. Anyone infected with a virus of this kind may die at any time."

"Thank you."

She got up and walked out of the clinic.

Forty.

Tim was preparing to go to work this morning when his phone rang. He received the call.

"Hello?"

"Hello Tim, this is Shawn."

"Hi Shawn, how is it going?"

"I have successfully obtained the search warrant and I am ready to visit your wife's house to conduct a search."

"Great. Let me know how everything turns out."

"Okay. I'll keep you posted."

"Thanks Shawn,", Tim said and hung up.

Angelina and Brian were in the house. They had not gone anywhere all day. She was very upset about being infected by the HIV virus. In her mind, she strongly felt that Brian may have had some affair while she was in Manila. She felt she had to confront him about this matter. This was a serious thing that could not have gone unanswered.

"The doctor just informed me that I have the HIV virus," Angelina said to Brian.

"What virus?"

"HIV, the virus that causes AIDS."

"HIV? You mean to tell me you have HIV?"

Angelina felt as if Brian was trying to accuse her of having the virus and never told him anything about it. She felt that this was an attempt to manipulate her and yelled out all the more.

"I got it from you."

"Not from me. No way. I don't have HIV."

"Where then did I get it from if not from you?"

"I don't know. From the Philippines may be. But I don't have HIV."

She paused for a while and began to cry, bending her head toward her knees. Brian sat quietly, not paying too much attention to her.

"When I was in Manila, I never had sexual intercourse with anyone. The doctor told me that the only way I would have contracted the virus was if I had sexual intercourse with someone who has the virus or is a drug addict, especially those who share needles in the course of drug use."

He stood up, trying not to look at her, yet he felt that she might know something about him. He wondered in his mind if she perhaps knew that he used drugs or ever had sex with another woman when she was away, but he wasn't sure. He was convinced in his mind that she had no clue of what had happened in her absence.

"I never had sex with anyone else, nor do I use addictive drugs, such as crack or cocaine."

At that very moment, Brian was in possession of crack, cocaine and the drug needle in his pocket. He was planning to go meet Bridget before this whole issue came about.

Immediately after he finished talking, Angelina kicked his leg and slapped him in the face. He ducked as she attempted to slap him a second time. He had never seen her this violent before.

"Honey, wait a minute. Why are you doing this?"

"Wait a minute? Wait a minute my ass!" She began chasing him around. Brian opened the door in an attempt to escape the quarrel and ran outside.

Incidentally, Officer Shawn and his partner had just arrived and were walking toward Angelina's apartment when Brian was running away. He saw him running out from the apartment but did not know who he was.

"Stop right there," Officer Shawn said.

He stood staring at him. He was shocked and totally surprised. To his knowledge, neither he nor Angelina had called the police regarding this matter.

"Get back in your apartment," the Officer commanded.

He walked back into the apartment while officer Shawn followed him behind. Angelina stood inside by the front entrance door, putting her shoes on, getting ready to pursue Brian outside.

"Get back in your apartment and sit down." The other officer said to Angelina. They had no clue why the cops were there.

Angelina and Brian sat down. Brian looked at the police. He realized his attention was not on him at the time. He slowly took the crack cocaine out from his pocket and threw it behind the couch. The police did not see him.

"We are on a warrant."" Officer Shawn said.

He brought out a piece of paper from his pocket and showed it to them. It was a search warrant from the court. He flagged it in their face. They said nothing but stared at the paper. Brian thought for a moment and asked, ""What for?"

"I'll let you know when we are done," Officer Shawn said.

The other officer had his gun drawn while Shawn was already searching around the apartment. He looked behind the couch and saw something wrapped around in a small waterproof bag. He picked it, opened it and saw vials of crack cocaine inside. He showed it to Angelina and Brian and said, "What is this?"

"I don't know," Brian said very quickly.

Angelina was still staring at it. She hadn't seen either cocaine or crack before and had no knowledge of what it was or how it looked, although she had heard of it and knew that people used it to get high, and more often than not, become addicted to it.

"I don't know," she said.

The cops immediately handcuffed them. One the officers began searching Brian's pockets. He found a pipe similar to the one Tim's son had for a toy as well as an injecting needle in his inner jacket pocket. He took it out, looked at it, and showed it to Brian.

"This looks like the pipe used to smoke crack. What is this doing in your pocket?"

Angelina was taken aback and confronted Brian in a loud voice, "You are a drug user??"

"Quiet please," the officer said to her. They arrested Angelina and Brian and drove them to the precinct.

They were sent to the Central Booking where they were held, awaiting to appear before the judge the following day.

Forty-one.

Officer Shawn called Tim and his phone rang. Tim answered.

"Hello?"

"Good afternoon, Tim. We conducted a search and found some crack cocaine in your wife's apartment. We also found some needles used for injecting heroin on her boyfriend Brian."

"What?" Tim screamed.

"We arrested the two of them. They are at the Central Booking unit, waiting to see the judge on a first appearance."

"Really? So my child has been exposed to drugs all along... Thanks Shawn, for the information, and congratulations for a work well done."

"You bet."

Tim hung up the phone and thought for a moment. He was disturbed about the fact that his son may have been exposed to drugs. The question he had for himself now was what could he do next. He thought it was alright to inform his lawyer. He dialed his attorney.

"Hello?"

"Hello, Mr. Lorluk. This is Tim Branch."

"Hi Tim!"

"I just got news that my wife and her boyfriend have been arrested. They are currently being detained at the Central Booking unit."

"Why? Do you know?"

"As per the information I provided to the Child Protective Services and the police, a search warrant was obtained and given to the police in order to search her apartment. The police found a good amount of crack cocaine and other drug paraphernalia in her apartment."

"This information will be good evidence to use against her in court. If you desire, we can fight for the sole custody of your child."

"I am scheduled to return the child to her next week, and now she is in prison."

"She is a first-time offender and may be released soon on bail, but we can file an injunction asking the court to put on hold the order of custody that was granted to her initially based on this new development."

"That's a good idea. When can this be done?"

"We can do this any time before the date you are scheduled to return your son back to her."

"You can proceed with the process. Bill me and I'll take care of your fees."

"Okay, I'll get on it right away."

"Thank you. I'm looking forward to that." Tim hung up. He felt relieved. He felt he had a good shot at getting full custody of his son. He was really in a good mood.

He took his phone out from his pocket and dialed Pamela. Her phone rang and she answered.

"Hello?"

"Hi Pamela, are you back yet?"

"In a way, yes."

"What do you mean?"

"I'm still not settled in my mind. I'm constantly thinking about the business. My brother keeps encouraging me to move forward."

"I'm glad you have someone like him. Someone to encourage you. That's a good thing."

"Yes. By the way, I forgot to tell you that I went over a nail and it punctured my tire. I had to call the emergency roadside. They came and towed it."

"That's unfortunate. You should have called me. I would have been right there to replace it."

"Really? Can you fix a flat tire as well?"

"I can do a lot of things when it comes to you, and that includes replacing a flat tire."

"Thanks. I appreciate that."

"Have you gotten the car back yet?"

"No."

"Hope you don't have to be late on that very important day."

"I won't. I'll just stay here alone until my brother comes."

"Must you wait for him?"

"No."

"Why don't you come over? I can keep you company. You can spend some time with me while you wait for your vehicle."

"That's a good idea, and even more so, very nice of you. Try all you can to expedite the process so we can seal the deal."

"I'll jump on it. You bet that at your command it's done."

"Oh. You are such a great guy Tim."

"I hope it will all work out for us."

"Well, we'll wait and see."

They hung up. Tim felt like a little boy who had just gotten a new toy from his mother.

Forty-two

Mr. Lorluk went to the family court. He had to file an injunction for a court interference regarding the order which granted Angelina custody of her son. He wanted the court to reverse the order, taking away child custody from her, and granting it to Tim.

Mr. Lorluk arrived first to the court and waited for Tim to arrive. Tim was running late due to heavy traffic condition. He decided to call Mr. Lorluk to inform him.

"Hello Tim."

"Hello Mr. Lorluk. I'll be running late but will be there soon."

"Fine. In the meantime, I'll be filing the necessary documents needed to get the action started."

"Thank you."

"I'll see you shortly."

Mr. Lorluk walked up to the court clerk and got the papers he would need to file the motion. He filled it out completely, leaving no question unanswered and submitted it to the court clerk, paying the filing fee. The case was placed on the court calendar for hearing.

Tim arrived in time before the court was ready to call his case. He walked inside the hearing room with his attorney. The case was ready to be heard.

"All rise!"

The court officer shouted as the judge walked in, and everybody in the courtroom stood up.

"You may now be seated."

They all sat down, and the judge was ready to address the case.

"This case is Tim Branch VS Angelina Branch. May the Defendant please stand?"

Tim's attorney immediately stood up and said to the Judge, "Your honor, the Defendant is not here and will not be able to attend."

"Do you have any idea why she is not here?"

"Yes your honor. She's currently incarcerated. I have the documents to prove that."

He handed the documents he obtained from the Central Booking department to the Judge, showing that Angelina was held there for a pending court appearance. The Judge glanced at it and gave it back to him.

"May I see your motion please?"

He handed the motion to him. He read the motion and placed the paper on his table.

"If I understand sir, you are seeking a motion asking this court to deny the Defendant Angelina Branch the right to custody of her son Tim Branch Jr. Is that right?"

"Yes your honor."

"On what grounds?"

"Your honor, the Defendant is currently incarcerated in a federal facility for a drug possession pending trial. When the police searched her apartment on a warrant, they found several ounces of crack cocaine in the premise. Her boyfriend, who lives with her, was also in possession of some heroin. They were both arrested and are held in separate jail cells as we speak, pending the outcome of the case. Such premise is unfit for a child to dwell in. Such people are unfit to raise a child in a safe environment."

The Judge picked up the papers from his desk and looked over it a second time and said, "I will place a temporary suspension on the previous order pending the outcome of the case with the Defendant, Angelina Branch. I hereby grant the Plaintiff, Mr. Timothy Branch, temporary custody of his child Timothy Branch Jr. The previous order awarding Angelina Branch custody of

Timothy Branch Jr. is temporarily suspended. This order is final."

"Thank you honor," Mr. Lorluk said.

He walked out of the courtroom with Tim happy and relieved.

Forty-three.

It was time for Tim to send his son back to Angelina, who was still in prison, awaiting to see the judge. The hearing was set for tomorrow. She thought it wise to call her friend Kikwana.

She dialed her number from the prison pay phone.

"Hello?"

A recorded message came on, "This call is from a federal detention facility. You will not be charged for this call. An inmate Angelina Branch is attempting to reach you. To accept press 1, to decline press 5, or simply hang up."

Kikwana was surprised to hear the recording. She didn't believe it for a minute. She pressed one to accept the call.

"Hello?"

"Hello Kikwana, it's Angie."

"Where are you?"

"The Police came to our apartment with a search warrant and searched the entire apartment. They found some crack cocaine and heroin on Brian and arrested us. We are being held at the Central Booking facility, waiting to appear in court soon."

"I know for sure you don't use drugs. Does he do drugs?"

I have no idea whatsoever. I was shocked and very surprised. In any case, we are here in prison for now."

"Can you post a bond? I'm convinced that you will be released if you post a bond since this is your first offence."

"I hope so, but right now, I'm concerned about my son, who is scheduled to be brought back to me tomorrow, the same day I'll be going to court for the bond hearing. Will you be able to pick him up from his father for me?"

"Yes. I'll go over there tomorrow and get him."

"Thank you."

"What time is your bond hearing?"

"11.00 a.m."

"Good time. I'll come to the court hearing in case they need someone for a guarantor."

"Thank you."

"You are welcome. I'll call your husband to inform him that I will be coming to see him by 7.00 a.m. in the morning so he can have your son ready by the time I get there."

"Thank you."

"By the way, does he know that you are there?"

"No. I have the order of protection against him so we do not have contact with each other."

"That's right. I almost forgot about that. I'll see you tomorrow in court."

"See you then."

They hung up. Kikwana was very unhappy and frustrated to learn of what was happening to her friend. But she had no control over it. She could only do whatever she could to assist her in this time of need. She picked up her phone and dialed Tim. His phone rang and he answered.

"Hello?"

"Hello Tim? This is Kikwana, Angelina's friend. She just told me to pick up her son tomorrow. She may not be able to make it there herself. Please have him ready before 7.30 in the morning. I expect to reach there by that time."

She didn't want him to know that she was in prison, and he acted as if he didn't know anything about her situation.

"Why can't she?"

"I can't answer that. She just wanted me to do her this favor. Please have him ready for me by then. I have other appointments after that."

"He'll be ready by that time. As a matter of fact, if you want, you can pick him today. I'll be here all day."

"Okay, that sounds even better. I should be there in three hours. Is that fine with you?"

"Yes. I'll be waiting."

Tim was at work during this conversation. He checked the time and hurriedly finished the job he had on hand and left for home.

Kikwana left her house and drove straight to Tim's house to pick up Angelina's son. When she arrived, Tim opened the door and let her in. Tim Jr. was standing beside him holding his hand. Kikwana extended her hand to pat him on the head, but he ducked away.

"Hello cutie," she said.

He ran behind his father not uttering a word.

"Hello Tim," she continued.

"Hi. Welcome," Tim replied.

"I am here to pick him up."

Tim handed her some papers, around three pages in total.

"This is a court order reversing the old order. The court has awarded me temporary custody of my son. The documents I just gave you is the court order. You can give that to your friend when you see her."

She widened her eyes in disbelief.

"Okay Tim, I'll make sure she gets it."

"If she ever needs my help in any way, don't hesitate to ask."

"We'll do that."

She walked away disappointed, wondering what was happening.

Forty-four.

Pamela arrived at Tim's house. She rang the bell and
Tim Jr. quickly ran and opened the door as she walked
in. He was excited to see her, although they had not
met before. He held her by the leg and Pamela bent
down to cuddle him.

"Welcome. Come in. My daddy is over here."

"Thanks cutie," she said as she followed him to the
room where Tim was.

As Tim stood up to welcome her, she looked at his face
and said, "He's so cute. He looks exactly like you."

"Thank you. everybody says that."

Lissandra noticed that there was a guest in the house.
She walked up to them. Tim Jr. saw her, picked up his
toys, and ran over to her. They walked down to the
lower part of the house where they usually stayed. He
was used to being around her. They got along very well.
He didn't feel his father's absence whenever he was
with her.

Tim picked up Pamela's bag and took it to the next
room where he intended her to sleep for the night. It
was the same room that Angelina lived in during the
time they lived together. He had replaced the mattress,
the bed sheets, and the pillow shams after she moved

out, giving the room a fresh new look and design. Pamela walked around the room toward the bar on the right and said, "You look so happy."

"Yes. Knowing that you were coming made me feel that way. I'm just happy to see you."

"Thank you. I'm excited about the deal tomorrow."

She put her hands on his shirt and buttoned it, for his chest was almost visible while he grabbed her arm and pulled her closer. He had left it open to draw her attention.

"Would you like something to eat?"

"Yes. I got a little hungry after I got off the air plane. Let me see if I can find something in your refrigerator to cook."

She walked over to the kitchen and opened the refrigerator. She looked inside it and shut it close."

"You should ask me to cook for you."

"That's really cute, but don't trouble yourself for now. I'll be fine with a little wine and some pie."

She went over to the living room, picked up the bottle of wine and opened it. She took the pie on the table, cut some of it, and put it on a silver plate.

They shared the pie together and they drank mildly. The wine was non-alcoholic.

"It feels so good to be around a person like you, having left my boyfriend after a long-term relationship."

"I feel just as you do. I got the child custody taken care of. My next move will be to proceed with divorce."

"How will that work now that she is not here?"

"I hope she wouldn't be there. Her absence will make the whole thing much easier, just as my lawyer told me not to worry about that."

"Getting rid of my boyfriend was not an easy decision. I understand exactly what you are going through. My family and very close friends were all involved. They wanted us to stay together, but in the end, I had to make a decision."

"I am sure you made the right decision. I am glad you made the right choice."

"At the end of this transaction, my mind will be free, settled and relaxed. I hope we can find more time to spend together."

"I'm looking forward to that and waiting impatiently, and hope we can find more time together."

They sat silently for a moment. Tim dialed his office to check on them. He knew things were going on as usual. Monica was there and she must have completed every document they needed to get the deal taken care of tomorrow.

"My office has already prepared every document that we will need for the transaction. A transaction like this is typically easy, especially when we have completed the audit. That's the difficult part of the job. But we are ready and set to proceed."

"Audits are a difficult part of a job. I am glad I have someone like you who makes it seem so easy."

"I am an accountant. I've learned to walk the hard line, bringing things to a simplified conclusion."

"You seem to have confidence in the job you do; that's what I like in a man."

"It's not just about confidence alone, but also about the love of job. That's what excites me the most."

"Some people work for the money. They are not concerned much about the job itself."

"That's why most people don't succeed in business. See how successful I have become."

"You are right."

It was getting late in the evening. They were tired and decided to call it a night. They couldn't see anything wrong with each other. They kissed each other good night and went to their respective rooms.

Forty-five

Kikwana arrived in court one hour earlier than
scheduled and sat down inside the hearing room.
Moments later, Angelina and Brian were brought into
the court room in handcuffs. The court officers held
them by their hands as they walked to the sitting area.
Angelina was seated and uncuffed. She turned around
and saw Kikwana sitting in the room. She smiled at her,
feeling a bit comfortable to know that someone was
there for her. Kikwana, on the other hand, didn't look
so happy seeing her in that humiliating situation, but
she got up and signaled the officer that was guarding
her that she wanted to talk to her before the hearing
was to begin and she began walking toward them.

"That's my friend," Angelina said to the officer.

"Okay," the officer said and slid over a little bit, giving
them room to speak.

The judge had not entered the courtroom as of yet. It
would take about thirty minutes before he was ready;
therefore, they had plenty of time to converse.

She took out the court order that granted Tim
temporary custody of their son and handed it over to
her.

"Your husband has been granted temporary custody of your son by the court. This order gave him the right to keep your child, pending the outcome of your case."

Angelina looked surprised and wondered how Tim knew she was arrested with her boyfriend. She began to think of this as a plot.

"How did he know that I am here?" she asked.

"I don't know," Kikwana said. "When I called him to arrange for a time to pick up your son, he invited me over to his house, and when I arrived, he asked me to give this document to you. I read it and walked away from him."

"Not a problem. He's his father any way. I just hope and pray that he's fine."

"He is fine, that I can tell you. He looks very happy with his father."

"Well, that's settled for now. I guess I have to deal with that when I get out. My main concern now is getting out of here."

"You will. After all, you don't use or sell drugs."

"You know that for sure, but they don't. Don't forget that they found some cocaine on the floor."

"That's not enough evidence to keep you here. Perhaps the judge will grant you bail, pending the outcome of the trial."

As soon as she had finished making this statement, the Judge was ready to make his entry into the courtroom. She walked back over to her seat and sat down. He walked into the courtroom and the court officer welcomed him, "All rise!"

Everybody in the room stood up until the judge was seated.

"You may now be seated," she said, and everybody in the room sat down as instructed.

The court did not waste any time in hearing the cases. It was now time for Angelina and Brian. They were instructed by the court officer to stand up and raise their right hand. They stood, raised their right hand, and were ready to take the oath.

"Angelina Branch, do you swear to tell the truth, the whole truth, and nothing but the truth?"

"Yes, your honor," she said and sat down.

"Brian Steeler, do you swear to tell the truth, the whole truth, and nothing but the truth?"

"Yes your honor" he said and sat down.

"You are charged with five counts of possession of drugs and endangering the life of a minor. How do you plead Mrs. Branch? Guilty or not guilty?"

"Not guilty."

The judged quickly researched her files and saw that this was the first time she was charged with a crime, and most first-time offenders usually get bail at the discretion of the judge.

"You will be granted bail today in accordance with the law. Your bail is set for $250,000.00 and can be posted in cash, certified check, or money or with any other acceptable non-cash assets."

"Mr. Steeler, guilty or not guilty?"

"Not guilty."

He looked at Brian's file and found out that that he had been arrested many times and had been in and out of jail several times.

"Mr. Steeler, you will not be granted bail. The court records show that you were charged with similar crimes several times before and are not eligible for bail. This court is adjourned."

Kikwana quickly walked up to Angelina. She looked stunned as to how much the bail was set for. It was a huge sum for a crime she thought was just a minor one.

"How do you hope to post this bail?"

"This is simply too much for me. I cannot do it now. Tim and I are no longer together. Maybe I'll have to stay here pending the outcome. I know I will be vindicated."

Kikwana thought for a while and said, "I think you should let your husband know about this. After all, you have a child together. Maybe he can help."

"Tell him that you saw me and have given me the court papers."

"Okay, I will. I will get back to you soon." She left the courtroom, handcuffed, and was escorted back to the prison cell with Brian.

Forty-six.

Kikwana dialed Tim's number. His phone rang and he answered.

"Hello?"

"Hello Tim, this is Kikwana. I met Angelina in the court. She was charged with five counts of drug possession and endangering the life and welfare of a minor."

"I'm aware of it. Did she receive the document?"

"Yes, I gave it to her and she signed for it."

"Great. I'll need a copy of the receipt for my record."

"I'll get it over to you in time."'

"When is she getting out? Do you know?"

"She's held on a $250,000.00 bond. She can walk out of prison anytime she is able to post a bond."

"Does she plan to post a bond?"

"She indicated to me that she cannot make the bail. She neither has the money nor the assets to make such a bail. She really needs any help she can get. She really needs your help."

He paused for a while, thinking, "Isn't this the same woman who stole $1.5million from my bank account and transferred it out of the country?"

"What does she want me to do?"

"She will be happy if you can bail her out. I'm sure she will be counting on you."

He looked at his son and felt compelled to act. He realized that she was his mother, regardless of the circumstances.

"Alright, I'll take care of it."

"When?"

"Immediately."

"Thank you."

He drove straight to his office. He sat down calmly on his chair, waiting to have this conversation with Monica before he leave. He picked up the intercom phone and paged his secretary.

"'Monica, please make out a check in the amount of $250.000.00 payable to the clerk of the court."

"Okay," Monica said.

She pulled out the checkbook and prepared it in that amount just as he had instructed and gave it to him to sign. He looked it over to make sure everything was as it was supposed to be. He signed it and gave it back to her.

"You can take it to the bank to have it certified. It will be used for a bail bond and it has to be in the form of guaranteed fund. After that, you can take it to the criminal court downtown. Angelina is held there waiting to post the bond."

"Alright sir. I'm on the way."

Monica put on her jacket and went straight to the bank. The check was certified and she went straight to the criminal court and posted the bond on her behalf. Angelina was released from prison. Monica drove her home, went back to the office, and informed Tim of the progress.

Tim left the office after Monica returned from the court and went back home. Pamela was up and ready to go to the meeting. She sat relaxed in the living room, watching the morning news. Tim walked into the house straight to the living where she was sitting.

"Good Morning Tim," Pamela said.

"Good morning darling," Tim replied.

"You got up so early. I see you are an early riser huh!"

"Not always. Kikwana called me very early this morning."

"Who is Kikwana?"

"She is Angelina's good friend."

"About her?"

"No. About bailing her out. You can say yes. About her."

"You didn't tell me she is in prison. Would you mind telling me why?"

"It's a long story. You know how she stole my money – $1.5 million – and transferred it out to Manila. She paid the nanny less than she received from me and created all sorts of problems between us. But that's not why she is in prison. She is there for drug possession and child endangerment."

"And you actually bailed her out after all this?"

"Yes. We don't talk to each other. The order of protection is still in effect, but currently, I have the custody."

"Where is she now?"

"Monica told me that she drove her home. She had no money on her when she was arrested and had no means of getting home."

"You are a kind-hearted man, Tim."

"I've always been that way. I guess it's my nature."

"I'm glad that she's out. That can make the divorce process much faster."

"You are right. I never thought about that. I can't wait to get this over with."

"You did right. That was the right thing to do. I like men who always make the right move."

He smiled and looked at her straight in the eye.

"I'm sure you got a good hold on me."

"You better be sure, just watch and see."

Forty-seven

Angelina left prison on bail. She felt happy to be free, at least for the moment. She felt free at home, but was also lonely and scared. Brian would remain in prison. He was not granted bail and was pending trial. She wanted her son back. She took out some time and read the court order. She read it over and over again until she was familiar with its content, and she took note of the wordings. She knew she was in for a big challenge getting the child back, particularly now that she had faced charges for drug possession and child endangerment; if convicted, she would have to serve a long time in prison. She was confronted with a difficult decision and was hard-pressed.

"I gotta think about this," she said to herself, sitting down almost helplessly, with her hand holding her head, leaning on her palm. Suddenly her phone rang and she picked it up with reluctance.

"Hello?"

"Hello Angie. How are you doing?" It was Kikwana.

"Exhausted. What a time to spend in prison."

"I'm glad you are out, at least for now."

"For now? I hope I'll never have to go back there again."

"I hope so myself."

"I'm just worried about my son right now."

"I'm sure he is in good hands. He's with his father. The last time I saw him he looked really happy."

"That is good to know. But let's put that aside for now. I can't help but wonder how my apartment ended up being searched."

"I believe this is an inside job. Tim may have informed the cops about what was going on there."

"But how would he know that there were drugs in the house?"

"I wonder about that too. He knows you don't do drugs. It could have been your next-door neighbor as well. They may have smelt or sensed something when you were away and alerted the authorities."

"I don't think this has anything to do with my next -door neighbor. It has to do with Tim. He probably wants me to end up in jail because I left him."

"Probably. See how he quickly filed for child custody and got it. He probably wants you to spend all your life in prison so he can keep the child."

"That won't work. I'll fight him tooth and nail."

"I know a person who can help you. He can take him out quickly. He's ruthless and doesn't ask for much."

"Now you are talking. Let's get together soon and begin to work on it."

"He's out of town now on a job and will be back next month."

"Okay, we'll wait for him."

They hung up. She sat back down feeling good, hoping to successfully carry out her plan. After a little while, she fell asleep on the couch.

Meanwhile, Tim drove Pamela back home. They arrived at her house and walked in. She had forgotten to dress her bed when she last left the house. Her coffee mug was still in the sink uncleaned. He sat down in the living room area and she sat by the dining end.

"I feel like having a cup of tea," he said.

"Sure, you can help yourself out," she replied.

He walked over to the kitchen. The coffee was sitting on top of the table. He looked around for a cup but did not see one. He looked in the sink and picked up a cup and was about to rinse it off when Pamela walked toward him.

"You didn't have to do that. There are lots of clean cups over there."

"Where at?"

"Inside the cabinet. You can use any one of those. That one needed to be cleaned."

"I'm sure you are the only one in the house, Apparently, you used it earlier on, right?"

"Yes. I was hurrying to get out, so I left it unattended."

"It seemed you knew I was coming so you left it for me. I'll attend to it."

"Uhh Tim, you are so sweet."

"Thanks. I hope you'll continue to say this forever."

"Why forever?"

"I realized that's how long it will take us to separate."

She reached inside the cabinet, took out a new mug, and gave to him. Tim poured the hot water into it and dropped in tea leaves, waiting for it to dissolve.

"I'm a little exhausted," Pamela said.

"I'm sure you are. You've been up all day."

"I'm quite surprise I went this long without a break."

"Perhaps you need a little rest."

He moved over and she came closer, resting her head on his shoulder. He felt her nipples and repositioned himself better.

One hour later, his phone rang.

"Hello?"

"Hello, Mr. Tim. It's Mr. Lorluck."

"How is it going?"

"Pretty good. I have completed all the necessary documents needed to terminate your marriage."

"Great. I have been waiting to hear from you regarding that. How does it look?"

"It's a pretty simple thing. The rules are clear. Everything you own together will be divided in half."

The house will not be divided since you bought it before you were married, and the $1.5 million that she wired out of the country will be deducted from the settlement."

"What about the child? That's my primary concern."

"The child, of course, has been settled already. You currently have temporary custody. However, I worked it out in such a way that you may be granted sole custody, but she will be given the right to supervised visitation."

"That sounds good. I hope the court agrees with us."

"It's most likely that they will agree with us, taking into consideration her current situation with the law."

"Thank you, sir."

"See you there."

Forty-eight.

Brian appeared in court in handcuffs. He couldn't afford bail nor could he afford a lawyer. Angelina showed up on her own with Kikwana without an attorney. The court appointed a lawyer who would represent them. The police officers who arrested them were also present. The prosecutor had all the evidence he needed to plead his case. Everybody in the courtroom had been seated and the trial was ready to begin. They sat beside their court-appointed attorney and the trial was set to start. Brian was questioned first.

"Mr. Steeler, you were charged with five counts of drug possession and endangering the life of a minor, is that correct?" the Judge asked.

"Yes, your honor."

"Were you in possession of the said drugs when you were arrested?"

"Yes, your honor, but I had no intention to sell them."

"What were your intention with the said drugs if you did not intend to sell them?"

"I intended to use them."

"When you say you intended to use them, what do you mean?"

"I don't understand your question."

"What were you using them for?"

"Oh, sorry your honor. I mean snort and smoke them."

"You mean to shoot the cocaine by injecting it in your body or through the nose?"

"I do both."

The Judge breathed down and sat back. He continued.

"Alright, there were some other drugs found on the floor of your apartment. Tell me about that."

Angelina was very nervous when she heard this question. She didn't know how he would respond to this. She paid particular attention to him.

"I'll be very honest with you your honor. The apartment does not belong to me. It's my girlfriend's apartment. We were arrested together. The drug found on the floor of the apartment fell off from my pocket when I tried to duck from the cops."

Angelina looked relaxed having heard this from him. She heard what she was hoping for. She appeared relieved. She knew this would help her case.

"If I understand very well, your girlfriend, in this case, is the co-defendant, Angelina Branch. Is that right?"

"Yes, your honor."

"Do you and Mrs. Angelina Branch usually snort and smoke cocaine?"

"No your honor. She never knew I did drugs."

All right Brian. I appreciate your being honest to this court. That will help me in making my judgment.

The clerk handed the Judge a document which contained Brian's prior arrest record. He looked at it, made his notes, and was ready to make a judgment

"Angelina, Brian has testified to this court, and after listening to him, I believe his statements are true. You will not be charged for the cocaine that was found in your apartment. You must be careful to know the kind of people you associate with. All the charges against you have been dropped."

She jumped up in jubilation and sat back down as tears of joy began to drop down from her lashes. Her lawyer tapped her on the back.

"Brian. I have looked at and carefully examined your criminal record. You could receive up to twenty-five years in prison. But because you were honest in all your answers, you have saved the court the time and cost it normally takes to prosecute a case. I hereby sentence you to ten years in prison, which is less time served. This court is dismissed."

Angelina could not hold back her tears when she heard this decision. She cried bitterly because she loved him so much. They looked at each other straight in the eyes as Brian was being led out of the courtroom in handcuffs. She walked out of the courthouse, a free woman.

"He thought I would go to prison," she said.

"That was his wish, but look, you are free," Kikwana replied, laughing and holding hands with her.

"My next move is to go to court and fight to get my kid back from him.""

"That's the next thing, but wait until the hit man returns. That will be a good time to do that."

"Yes. I'll send him to serve the papers. He can shoot and kill him there."

"He knows his job. Perhaps, he got a better idea."

"You are right. We just have to give him the job and leave it up to him. We haven't really discussed what I'll get out of this. You know I have been behind you from the start and I'll be thrown out of my apartment soon for not paying rent."

"What about $50,000.00 in cash?"

"$50,000.00? You'll have to inherit a lot."

"That's right. You know I have a son to take care of as well."

"I never really thought about that. But we are talking about millions here."

"You're right girl. You've being with me from day one. $100,0000 will be just fine."

"Okay. That's a deal. I'll settle for that."

"What about the hit man?"

$10.000 is all he need. The last time I had him break this guy's legs, he only wanted $5000.

"That's fine. If all goes well, I'll double it for him."

"I'm sure he'll appreciate it. I just hope this get done before the divorce hearing."

"It will."

"You know what else I think?"

"What?"

"Since you're going to lose your apartment soon, why don't you come live with me till?"

"I think that's a good idea. We don't have to travel back and forth or talk on the phone. You never know who is listening. I'll make place for you to stay."

She moved into her apartment and waited until the hit man returned. That could take a few months, but they hoped he would be back on or before the divorce court date to carry out the plot.

Forty-nine

The case for divorce was scheduled for today. Tim and Angelina hadn't seen each other for two years since she moved out of the house. The case was scheduled to be heard in the evening. Tim went to work as usual and would head to the court house later in the evening with his attorney for the divorce hearing.

He arrived at work and was ready to conduct his business as usual.

"Monica, have you heard anything from them regarding the bid?"

"Not yet, but I'm hoping to hear from them shortly, before noon, as I was told."

"Okay, thanks."

He felt restless this morning and wasn't quite sure why he felt that way. He had never felt this way before in the past. Sometimes, he felt miserable and uneasy or awkward , and scared. He picked up the phone and called his lawyer to get an idea of what the outcome of the case would look like.

"Hello?"

"Hello sir, it's Tim."

"Hi Tim."

"I'm just trying to get an idea of what we will be expecting to hear from the Judge today."

"Based on your net worth, I have calculated that the court may award her $25 million in cash settlement, and that's being fair."

"That's fine with me. I'm mostly concerned about our child. I'll be relieved when it's all over."

"I know it won't hurt you much. You'll make it up in the future. But regarding your son, you may get joint custody unless the Judge concludes that she is not fit to raise a child."

"I hope so. I feel blessed in many ways. I didn't lose much. I have a son by her and I am now in a new relationship."

Tim looked at his watch. It was time to go to the court. He was anxious to get there. He just wanted to get it over with.

"I guess we have to start heading over there now. I am going there as soon as we hang up."

"I'm on my way as well. We'll meet up there."

They hung up and headed to the court.

Tim arrived first in court and sat inside the hearing room. His attorney arrived three minutes later and sat behind him. The judge walked in and all were seated. Angelina had not appeared and the Judge was ready to proceed with the case. Tim looked back and forth to see if his wife was there, but did not see any sign of her.

Suddenly, he heard shoes squeaking on the floor as if someone on a high-heeled shoe was walking so fast to make it into the room in a hurry. It sounded familiar to him, like that of Angelina's. He knew she loved high-heeled shoes.

He turned his head backward toward the entrance of the door and saw Kikwana walking into the court room. He felt relieved. He suspected Angelina was with her, following behind. But she walked straight to the front desk where he and his lawyer were sitting facing the Judge and stood in front of the Judge.

"Are you Angelina Branch?" the Judge asked.

"Angelina is dead," she replied.

"She is dead?"

"Yes, she is dead," she said, as she handed an envelope to the judge. He opened it and inside was a death certificate from the hospital where she was taken to confirming her death.

"I have here in front of me the death certificate of Angelina Branch," the judge said and passed over the certificate to Mr. Lorluck, Tim's attorney.

He looked at it and showed it to Tim. He read it in disbelief and gave it back to his attorney. He accepted it and walked up in front of the judge.

"Your honor, since the defendant in this case is now deceased, I hereby withdraw the case on behalf of the Plaintiff."

"Your request is granted. Case withdrawn."

Tim walked out of the court in tears, shaken and in disbelief. He got inside his car and turned on his cell phone. He had switched it off when he was in the court room to avoid interruption. Immediately, his phone rang.

"Hello?" he answered.

"They have accepted your bid and have awarded you the contract for $125 million," Monica said in jubilation.

"Thanks for the information. That is good to know, but Angelina just passed away."

"What?"

"I'm heading to the hospital right now to see her. I will talk to you soon."

He hung up and drove straight to the hospital where she died. When he arrived there, he met the nurse who attended to her and introduced himself.

"Hello dear, I'm Tim Branch, Angelina's husband," he said softly.

"Welcome sir."

"Thank you."

"She was brought into this hospital late last night, complaining of cold. She died later this morning of complications from pneumonia and AIDS-related infections."

She took him into the room where her body lay. He looked at her and wept bitterly. He kept it a secret from his son until her deceased body was released to him. They mourned her for thirty days and buried her in a local cemetery.

The news of her death reached Brian in prison. He loved her so much that he wanted to spend the rest of his life with her. He mourned her death with fellow inmates. He died thirty days in prison following her death of complications from AIDS.

ABOUT THE AUTHOR

JJ Mofus lives in New York City. He enjoys sailing and piloting, and is delighted to hear from his readers.

www.ingramcontent.com/pod-product-compliance
Lightning Source LLC
Chambersburg PA
CBHW021459110726
47899CB00001BA/220

* 9 7 8 0 6 9 2 9 0 7 1 8 4 *